Snow in PUERTO RICO

Snow in PUERTO RICO

LEO SMITH

iUniverse LLC
Bloomington

Snow in Puerto Rico

iUniverse books may be ordered through booksellers or by contacting:

iUniverse LLC
1663 Liberty Drive
Bloomington, IN 47403
www.iuniverse.com
1-800-Authors (1-800-288-4677)

ISBN: 978-1-4917-0330-4 (sc)
ISBN: 978-1-4917-0331-1 (ebk)

Library of Congress Control Number: 2013914679

Printed in the United States of America

iUniverse rev. date: 08/23/2013

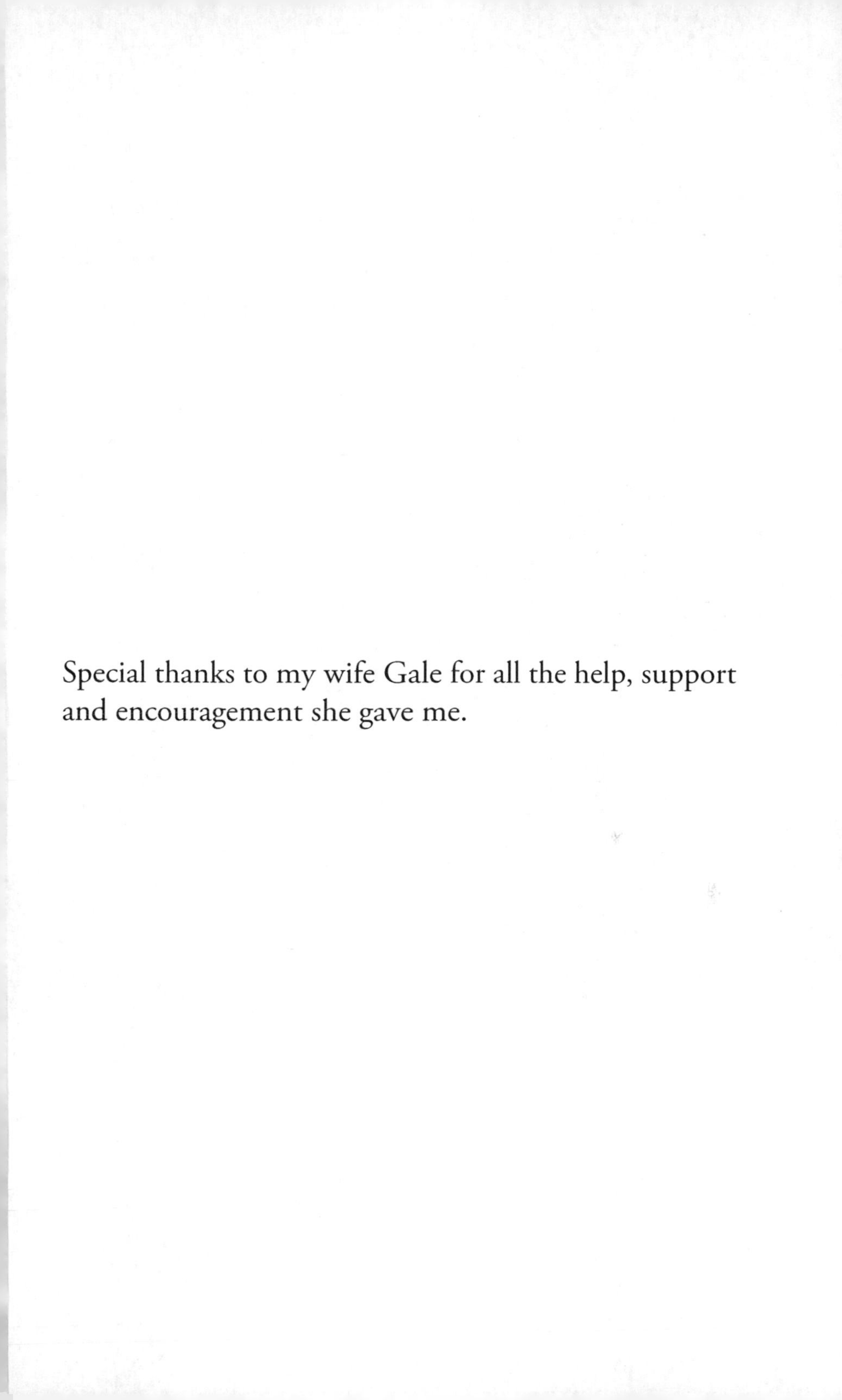

Special thanks to my wife Gale for all the help, support and encouragement she gave me.

Chapter 1

The clouds were pure white and it looked like we were drifting over snow. The sky above was as blue as it could be for a clear day. I could see the clouds forming white castles and mountains as they passed by rapidly. All of a sudden we started going downhill. The sky looked strange when we left all the white clouds behind. We now could see the blue sea below us with its white caps. A freighter was slowly moving toward its destined port. I was in flight back to the island, back to Puerto Rico. It's snowing in Puerto Rico they said in Washington because of the cocaine trade.

My name is Robin Perez and I am a Special Agent. My father and my mother are from New Mexico of Spanish ancestry from Castilla la Vieja, Spain. They were mostly ranchers raising cattle. My grandparents came to America in search of a better life. I was born in New Jersey when my father was a soldier stationed at Fort Dix. After he came back from World War II we moved around to several military posts on the U.S. mainland. He was then transferred to Germany where we spent several years and saw the reconstruction after the war. Just before his retirement he was transferred to Fort Buchannan, Puerto Rico. There I finished high school and went to college graduating with a Bachelors Degree in Social Science and received my R.O.T.C. commission.

After advanced officers school, I went to Vietnam as an infantry advisor. No sooner did things change and I was in the field with my own platoon. I saw everything from prostitution to how men got hooked on drugs. I made up my mind to remedy this problem. After I got discharged I went to work with U.S. Customs. There we were searching for contraband, mostly drugs, coming into the United States. I later transferred to the Bureau of Narcotics. I spoke Spanish fluently and had knowledge of the territory so that's why I am on my way down Puerto Rico.

As I was looking at the ocean I started thinking about the past few months in D.C. Serving as an adviser and instructor for special agents was a great honor but I was more of a street person than a desk jockey. It brought back memories of when I started as a rookie agent for US Customs and I went through the same routine over and over (classroom, shooting and pt). Walking the streets of D.C. was interesting and dangerous.

While in Washington I had liked going to the Ramada because of the musicians that were playing. Jody was the lead singer with Phil. Jody was tall with long black hair, beautiful green eyes and a great body as well as voice. On the breaks Jody sat our table and we talked about music, drinks and different things. It was nice to have a good conversation with someone other than co-workers. Three of us were usually together, Thomas Whitehorse and Francisco Delgado, alias Pancho Villa. Thomas was a full-blooded Suix Indian who works as a Federal Reservation Police mostly in the North Dakota area. He was always eating beans and loved to drink beer. Francisco was from the" Mexican Federales" on loan to us. He was the gourmet of the group and always carried his friend, a bottle of "Jose Cuervo".

I came back to reality when the flight attendant came by. She had a nice smile and charming personality. She was blond, about 5'8" and probably in her late twenties. She came by offering us lunch. They said it was "arroz con pollo" (rice and chicken) but it tasted more like rubber chicken with instant rice. The beans reminded me of Whitehorse and I ate half of them in his honor.

They were the proteins I needed anyway. The flight attendant had no tequila so I just had a Budweiser beer.

I quickly fell asleep and had a good nap. An hour must have passed when I felt the turbulence moving the airplane up, sideways and down. It felt quite bumpy. After flying so many times I knew we were descending. The lights came on to fasten your seat belts. The lady next to me and her daughter were fast asleep and covered with a blanket. The flight attendant came by checking on everyone making sure they had fastened their seat belt. She woke the lady and her daughter up to make sure they were buckled up. We kept descending slowly. We could see some boats on the dark blue ocean clearly. One was a cruise ship coming into port and the others were small motor boats and sailboats. The water turned different colors from blue to clear green.

We descended closer to the water and we could see the island at a distance. We could see the vegetation turning from light green to dark green, which meant there had been some rain. We could see some of the old houses with aluminum rooftops and a few concrete houses. As we approached we started seeing office buildings and apartment houses. The Island was only 110 miles long and 35 miles wide with a population of about four million. San Juan, the capital, had about half million. The briefing in Washington painted an aggressive picture full of daily shootings and killings. They told me to be careful of the local police. They are not trustworthy. I got myself into this mess by being a little bit more aggressive and hotheaded in my previous assignments. They had read me the riot act which means "You must behave while you are there Robin or else". Finally we reached the runway approach. Just as we were touching down the lady and her daughter sitting next to me made the sign of the cross and started praying. I heard other persons doing the same thing. It was customary in the Latino culture. The touchdown was uneventful like we wanted and everyone gave the captain and crew their approval by applauding and cheering. The aircraft taxied to the main terminal.

CHAPTER 2

At the Bureau of Narcotics, Don walked out of his office and saw Jose at his desk. He asked, "I thought you and Andrew were going to the airport to pick up someone?"

Jose said, "Yes, I am waiting for Andrew. He is in the bathroom".

Don walked over to the bathroom and slowly opened the door. He found Andrew looking out the window with a transistor radio to his right ear and moving his left hand up and down real fast. Don sneaked up to him and said, "Come on Andrew. You guys were to be at the airport already". It was horse race day at "Hipodromo El Comandante" (Comandante Racetrack) and Andrew had placed a couple of bets.

Andrew turned off his little radio and said "Yes sir, sorry. We are on our way". Andrew and Jose got into their car and as they were leaving the parking lot flipped on the radio. They called into the base station with their call sign, "106, 107, 10-8" to let the base know their radios were operational.

Base responded "10-4" loud and clear.

It took some time to travel from Old San Juan to Isla Verde where the airport was. Traffic was slow. When passing the Lloren Torres apartments they saw police blocking the entrances. It looked like they were on a search operation. When they finally arrived at the airport, Andy got out of the car and walked to a corner of the terminal with his transistor. This was an important race, Battle Rage was racing and even though he was not the favorite he had the best chance to win. Jose stayed by the car looking at the passengers leaving the terminal. He was looking for Robin.

In the meantime, the plane was still moving slowly in order to hook up with the corridor to the terminal. People were already getting out of their seats looking for their carryon luggage. I could hear the crackle of paper bags and the moving of cardboard boxes as people said "Dame mi bolsa por favor". *(It is customary that Puertorrican's bring food and presents in paper bags and cardboard boxes because they did not have carryons).* Everyone was in such a hurry. I just sat there and waited until the rush died down. I grabbed my carryon and walked to the terminal. Suitcases were starting to come out of the conveyer and I spotted one of mine but I could not get to it. There were cardboard boxes and heavy loaded suitcases blocking the way. Finally, I could get one of my suitcases out. I knew my next suitcase would not be far behind. I helped an old lady pull out two large heavy boxes. She was bringing a microwave and some electrical components, which looked like stereo equipment. My second suitcase came up and I was on my way to the exit. The porter brought me right out to the taxi line. I looked around and not expecting a car to be picking me up. I got into the next taxi. I asked him to take me to the Hilton, which was near El Condado, the tourist section in Old San Juan. It was hot and muggy. I took out a cigarette and lit up.

Andrew came over to Jose and said, "well I got my money back plus ten extra dollars".

Jose just shook his head and said "I have not seen the person we are supposed to pick up come out here."

Andrew said, "I will check inside the terminal".

A few minutes later he came out and said "everyone from that flight has left the terminal. Call Don and ask him if he wants us to check the hotels".

Don requested that they both come back to the office.

My taxi ride turned out to be quite interesting. The radio in the taxi kept playing "Band on the Run" by Paul McCartney and Wings, like a broken record over and over. We passed the Lloren Torres residential project. We saw all hell had broken loose. Police cars were all over the place. People were running away from the projects and the police. "Band on the Run", the taxi driver said, meant the police were conducting a raid. The drug traffickers were on the run.

Chapter 3

When I arrived at the hotel the bellboy took my luggage to the front desk. I was lucky that they had a room since I had no reservation. My room was on the third floor with a small balcony facing the ocean. I stepped out to take a look at the contrast of blue and teal in the water with waves that followed as smooth rhythm ending up in white foam. The air had a salty mist with the sweet smell of sea weed. My luggage was brought up and I decided to unpack a few things and take a quick shower. I got dressed and loaded my revolver with bullets, and packed it on my left side. It was a small standard chief's special that was issued to me after basic training BN (Bureau of Narcotics).

I went down to the lounge and sat at a small table with my back to the wall in order to have a clear view of the bar and main entrance. I ordered a gin and tonic and pulled out a cigarette and lit up. I noticed that two tables away from me there was a woman sitting alone. She was playing with her long, light brown hair. At the same time she was looking back and forth looking for somebody. She was young, about 25 years old. She made eye contact with me and even cracked a smile. Then she looked at a tall dark hair man standing at the bar about twenty feet away from me. He was talking to another man that stared at me. I ordered a second gin and tonic. I noticed a third man that came in from the side door. He wore dark pants and a black shirt looking around frantically.

The waiter brought my drink.

The man dressed in black grabbed the woman sitting alone by the hair. He pulled her out of her chair saying "so cabrona que te estas creyendo"? (You stupid goat, what were you thinking).

I stood up immediately and said, "Hey you wait a minute". As I started to walk toward the man, the waiter stood in front of me and said "No senor, please do not interfere now".

I stood back as I saw the poor lady being dragged out of the lounge. As she got to the door she turned and gave me a glance. I started to push the waiter away and go after them, but the waiter insisted I stand back.

I sat back down and drank my gin and tonic. I asked the waiter why he stopped me.

The waiter said, "The two men at the bar are very good friends of the man that dragged the lady out. One of them I think pulled something out of his pocket that looked like a blade".

"And who was the lady" I asked?

The waiter responded, "She works the clubs you know. The man that took her out is her *chulo*".

"Yes, I know what you mean, a pimp. She is a *puta* right, a whore"? "Yes", he said.

That was enough information for me. The waiter just saved my skin. I walked over to the main restaurant in the hotel and I had the daily special which was sopa de pescado (fish soup) and the main course was arroz con gandules y pernil (red rice with pigeon peas and roasted pork).

After dinner, I walked out of the hotel. I turned left and walked across the "Dos Hermanos" bridge onto Ashford Avenue. This is where all the tourist hotels are located. I saw some unmarked police cars on the side of the road. About a dozen men were on the corner near the Condado Hotel. The police had five young guys lined up against the wall being searched.

I continued my walk for a while. I saw the two men that were at the bar in the hotel walking across the street. They went into a bar called "El Torreon". The bar was crowded and I was tempted to go in. But I decided to walk back to the hotel and stay out of trouble. Instead I walked over to the beach, took my off my socks and shoes rolling up the legs of my pants. I walked slowly in the surf as the waves cuddled my feet. I sat on a boulder and watched the Atlantic Ocean as it painted sunset sprinkles. The swift odor of salty iodine reminded of the days of R and R at China Beach when in Vietnam. Night came fast. It was a clear hot one and the full moon was high. It brought memories of her as we watched the waves talking to us and we made love under the moonlight glow. Her body was soft and white with her hair short with a sweet smell. She was a nurse assigned to the medical facility at the command post and we were to get married when we got back to the States. The Viet Cong were close to her camp and a mortar round fell on her tent. I didn't get the opportunity to accompany her body back home.

Chapter 4

The next morning I got a taxi ride to the Post Office located on "Recinto Sur "street. I walked up to the second floor, passed the U.S. Marshals office to the Bureau of Narcotics. When I opened the door I saw two young ladies at their desks. A lady with short dark hair and tan skin came over and greeted me with a nice warm smile.

"Good morning. I am Lidia. May I help you"?

"Yes. I am reporting for duty, my name is Robin Perez. These are my transit papers".

She took my envelope and asked me to sit down for a moment as she walked through a door to let them know that I was there.

A tall, strong man with short hair and a couple of scars on his face came out and said, "Welcome. Please come in. I am Don Stanwyck ". I followed him down the hall to his office. He asked me to have a seat as he sat down at his desk. He pulled out a cigarette and offered me one but I said no.

He said "Hope you had a good flight down. Would you like some coffee"?

I said "yes".

"Where are you staying?" Don asked.

I answered, "At the Hilton for the moment".

Lidia came in with two coffees.

He reviewed some papers and said "You have an impressive record. Your work in New York was commendable despite the hassle it caused the administrators".

Before I came on my trip I had to visit with the Director of Operations, ex-military Col. Stewart Harrington at our Washington Office who read me the riot act.

"You shot the Cuban and killed him. I know you were exonerated because it was considered self-defense", Don said.

"Yes sir, indeed it was", I responded. (*My partner and I were arresting three Cubans that were part of a ring trafficking in heroin. One of them started running and shooting at us. My partner got hit and I shot back and killed him).*

"You caused quite a scene in Atlantic City as well. You put away Tino Garcia and his gang of hoodlums. You sent Axel to the hospital with a broken arm and Tony with bruises all over", Don said.

"They resisted arrest after we did all we could to persuade them to . . ." Don interrupted me.

"No need to continue. I know the story", Don said.

"Nevertheless, I am glad you are here with us and I hope we have no incidents we have to regret later. You probably know this, but I am going to repeat it. The island gets hit by sea, air, and any other ways they can use to bring the drugs in so they can get them to the mainland. They call cocaine "*blanca nieve*" which is white snow. We have hard core heroin and marijuana in abundance. The policy in Washington for Puerto Rico is containment. They think if it manages to stay here we let the locals deal with it. Just avoid it getting to the mainland", Don said.

"I understand sir", I responded.

"The island could also be considered the murder capital of the USA. Two years ago we were averaging 35 murders a month. Last year it went up to 60 a month. This year it seems like it's going to be even higher. I would say that most of the murders are, in one way or another, drug related. I would like to get you settled in as comfortable as possible. You met Lidia, one of our administrative assistants. She will give you paperwork and some information on living quarters that might interest you. I will give you some briefs to read but first let me show you to your desk and the rest of the office".

After a tour of the office he introduced me to the rest of the staff. I met Andrew, a tall dark skinned man with an athletic build. Jose was medium height, slender with dark hair parted on the left side with a full mustache. Arnaldo was the shortest with a thin mustache, short hair and had the most experience. McIntire was medium height, brown long hair and the chubbiest. Joe was Puertorrican from NYC. Lidia was young, sweet and you would like her the moment you saw her. Marta, I noticed, was the more serious of the two women with long brown wavy hair and very well built. I was shown my desk and locker and was given a tour of the rest of the office.

I went back for a cup of coffee then sat at my desk reading the materials that Don had given me. I read that off the coast of Tumaco and sometimes Esmeralda, Colombia, they use a speed boat to bring the cocaine and marijuana to Manzanillo, Mexico. Sometimes they just meet a trawler at sea and transfer the merchandise and bring it in to San Diego. I knew about the air drops in Puerto Rico and also Dominican Republic. I found that the report said they were flying out of Monteria and sometimes Cartagena (Colombia) to Bahamas and from there it was an easy jump to Florida.

Joe came over to my desk and gave me a run down on the situation. I offered a cigarette and he took one.

"The caserios (public housing) are all points of distribution. Every now and then a new figure emerges as the leader of the point. The shootings are getting worse and the collateral damage increasing. These guys think that if they knock off the point man they can just move in and take over. That's where the trouble begins", Joe said.

CHAPTER 5

Next morning I was in the office at 0800 sipping some coffee when Don asked me to come in his office. Joe was there sitting looking over some papers.

"I want you to go with Joe to Vega Baja. There is a Woodstock-style festivity called "Mar y Sol" that started a few days ago. There are more than 10,000 people there. We know that there is a heavy concentration of cocaine and marijuana. It is coming from two sources and we want to confirm that Javier Montero from the Quintero Sinaloa gang and Angelo Selvaggio from New York are the major players. Joe will share some of the Intel we have and give you an up to date sit-rep," Don said.

I asked if we knew if these guys were there and if we were going to bring them in for questioning.

Don responded "I doubt that they are at the festival. But there will be enough info on their whereabouts. We do have a warrant for Montero, but as I said he is very elusive. Local police narc is keeping track of this. You might want to go down to their office. It's located at Camino Alejandrino, and speak to the Captain".

We gathered our stuff together. I took off my blazer and tie. I put them in my locker and pulled out my cuffs and gun.

Joe came by and said, "You probably can leave those cuffs here. I have some in the car that we can use."

Joe had a 1970 tan Impala and we drove out on Marina St. and as we turned to Fernandez Juncos Street Joe pointed and said "That dump is La Riviera Bar. It's a drug and prostitution hang out owned by some guy with connections in New York".

Further up on Fernandez Juncos street Joe said, "This is the holding facility, the stop 8 jail. They call it stop 8 because the public transportation bus stops at pier 8 which is right in front of the jail".

It was a cool morning for a change. We made a turn into "zona partuaria" the port zone which was the area where all inbound and outbound shipping was done. We passed the Bacardi factory, at which Joe said I could come any day and they would give me a free tour and some samples.

Joe Rodriguez was tall and muscular with dark curly hair. You could tell he worked out. Joe was originally from NY, Brooklyn of Puertorrican parents. He was doing a good job giving a site tour while I read the Intel report. We talked about the military. Joe served in Nam in 1966 and 68 in Camp Fay, Da Nang, with the Fast Boat Patrol. He was a quiet person and very observant. The Fast Patrol was the MAC-SOG element of the war. They were involved in spying and other spook stuff during that time. I didn't ask what he was tasked with during his Nam tour because I know the answer was classified. Many times the Fast Boat guys ran errands for the CIA.

Chapter 6

We drove past a large housing area called Levittown and on the right side we could see the ocean, calm with slow moving waves topped with lacy foam. There were a few picnickers out on the white sandy beach. We continued west on Rt. 2. This road was originally built by the military as a one-lane road so they could get their trucks moving during WWII.

We arrived at the town of Vega Baja. We had to park about a mile away from the festivities. Joe reported in on the radio and indicated we were going to walk to the main site. There was a big banner that said "*WELCOME TO FESTIVAL MAR Y SOL*". People were spread out in an area of about 400 acres. There was garbage all over the place and those who did not have a tent were sleeping on the ground. There were some people staggering around drunkenly. Some women and men were showering with a hose in the open field. I heard a mean tenor saxophone playing and I had no doubt it was Herby Mann. There were great performers there: B.B. King, the Allman Brothers band, Dr, John and many others.

Joe said "See those guys wearing guayaberas, shirts with four pockets. They are from the local police department. Let's stay away from them".

We continued walking trying not to step on anyone. As I happened to look inside a tent I saw a guy injecting himself, so I pulled Joe over.

I said, "Let me talk to the guy".

"Go right ahead, but I don't think it will do you any good", Joe responded.

I went in the tent and the guy got startled.

"Hey amigo I want some of your medicine for my pain", I said.

"I don't know what you are talking about", the man said. "You're invading my privacy", he repeated.

The guy babbled incoherently for awhile and then fell asleep. I searched and found some hell dust in small bags. The way it was cut and wrapped gave me a clue where it was coming from.

Joe said "let's leave this for the locals. It will be a good hit for them". He saw one of the locals and called him over.

We made our way through another group of highly inebriated people until we reached a tall man that was giving instructions to some other guys. We saw a man shouting out some orders to some workers.

"Hey buddy. Who's in charge here?" Joe asked.

"I am just with sanitation and cleanup of all these pigs. The boss is Miguel and left about an hour ago", the man said.

"Who is Miguel? I asked.

"Miguel Cuevas is the supervisor of the event", the man said.

"Is Javier or Tony around?" Joe asked.

"I don't know anyone by those names. Why don't you ask around if you can find someone sober or not high", the man said.

"Thanks pal", Joe said.

We continued to move until Joe stopped and said, "Oh shit"! He heard a voice say, "Oye viejo los federicos estan aqui tengan cuidado", (hey men careful, Federal Agents are here). I looked over and saw a short guy wearing a New York Yankee cap waving at us.

Joe said, "That is Lt. David Gonzalez and his panic squad. They are agents of the Criminal Investigations Bureau of P.R.

police. They love to show off and are knowledgeable but with a lot of bullshit".

I asked, "How do you know which is which"?

"You will soon see", Joe said.

"Hello Joe. How is everything"? David asked.

"Just fine David, how about you"? Joe asked.

A young woman came up to us and as she eyed us both she whispered something to David. She then turned to Joe waving a good morning as Joe did the same. She was in her early thirties light brown hair in a pony tail, beautiful green eyes and a figure that showed she worked out. She moved gracefully back to the search area. I could not keep my eyes off her.

David excused himself but before he moved said, "You have not introduced me to your new partner".

"He is Rob, Rob this is David".

"The pleasure is mine. Anytime you need any help give me a call or swing by our sub-office which is at walking distance from yours". David said.

"Hey, David could you come over here?" the young woman asked. "Sorry", David said. "That's Maranda. I think she needs me. Catch up with you guys later. Pleasure meeting with you".

"Well, I think we are about done here," Joe said. We were just turning back when David called us over.

"What do you have?" I asked.

There were two guys lying on the floor with their hands cuffed behind their backs. He had found two automatic pistols, a load of cash, white powder that could be cocaine and cannabis, one case of rum, whisky, gin and five cases of beer, and two cases of soda bottles. They all had military stickers from the Naval Base at Fort Buchanan. They were tax free for personal consumption only and not for sale.

The two guys on the ground were locals. We copied their information down.

David said, "It would be best for my team to take care of everything since there were several infractions".

On our way back to the office we decided to stop by the local police drugs and narcotics office at Camino Alejandrino, Guaynabo. It was an old building that must have been a big house at one time. The place was packed with people. While we were there a flatbed truck pulled up to the curb and the driver walked inside the office. He reported that on the bed of the truck there were 15 persons sitting and laying down, most of them smoking pot. The cops went out and escorted them into the holding cell

The local police had arrested two men originally from New York that worked for Selvaggio. We did get some Intel which led us right back to the same sources, Selvaggio and Montero. There was not much information on the men that worked for New York yet but their attorney was already on site.

Joe called Don and gave him a sit-rep to which he suggested we regroup at the office to consider the options.

We went over all the information with Don and we started to diagram where the drugs were coming from. There had been a recent drop of bags of cannabis in the town of Fajardo. There were also sightings of airplane drops in different areas of the island.

Montero is with the Sinaloa group in Mexico but also coordinates with the Rodriguez group. Don Manolo Rodriguez, known as the "Don" is the owner of *Rodriguez Sociedad Anónima de Transporte Internacional and Fruta-Vegetal Rodriguez Sociedad Anónima* in Colombia. Both are legitimate businesses in the fruit and vegetable field including transportation of the product. He is well respected and very well connected in government circles.

Jairo Cortes, known as Manga, and Rodolfo Madarriaga, known as Cuchilla, worked for Calixto Don Manolo's son. Rodolfo has some men working for him and they are all from Cali, Colombia.

Angelo Selvaggio, also known as "Gelo Lips", was a made man from the Gambino family in New York. When he comes to P.R. he socializes with Tony Turizzi owner of the Riviera Bar and also part owner of the Black Angus Bar.

Chapter 7

I was assigned a 1970 Dodge charger which was in very good shape and it had a quick response time. I decided to go and get a bite to eat at a restaurant called "Fornos" in Santurce. I had a "beefsteak encebollado con papas" (onion fried steak and fries) and a couple of Schlitz beers. After that I drove down to the Condado area and parked two blocks away from the Torreon Bar. I entered the bar and there were about 5 persons there. The bartender was a woman. She was about 30 years old, blond short hair, white and talked with an accent. She told me her name was "Gigi". I asked her where she was from and she said Argentina. I ordered a gin and tonic and sat there in silence for awhile observing a group of men that were talking and playing a game of dice. Obviously, they were not from the island. Their accents sounded either Colombian or Argentinean.

All of a sudden I saw a person enter the bar. He was 6 ft. tall and walked with a limp. I got off my stool to shake hands with him. It was my buddy from college, Rafael Estes also known as Bolin. We studied in UPR and got our ROTC commission together.

"Can I buy you a drink", I asked?

Bolin asked for a cubalibre and I also asked Gigi for another gin and tonic.

I asked, "What happened to your leg"?

"I was stationed at Firebase Bill, in the Pleiku area. We had some 155 Howitzers giving artillery support to the infantry and we got flanked by heavy mortars and rockets. I got hit by shrapnel and was med-evacuated. After lying in a hospital in Japan and with lots of therapy I was sent back to the states and given a desk job. They gave me a partial disability pension, which meant I could work. They put me on inactive reserve", Rafael said.

"I know what that was like. My squad was out on patrol when our main company camp got hit by a barrage of mortars. We lost our CO and our XO got severely wounded. It was a nightmare to get back to work again", I said

"So, what are you doing now? Are you retired?" I asked.

"I am a supervisor with US Customs at the San Juan pier going crazy with all the containers", Bolin said.

We exchanged cards and had some small shop talk. Bolin saw me looking at the group of men on the other side of the bar.

He said "most of them are from South America. Son chulo de puta. That was the local term for "pimps". They manage most of the foreign prostitutes and everything that comes with them in the area. If I were you I would not stare at them or even interfere in their games."

We talked for a while until the other guys started getting loud. I noticed that one of the guys was the same one I had seen leaving the Hilton with the woman. The dice game was rolling strong. There was a sizeable pot. I heard one of the guys say he rolled two pairs of three. More money went into the pot. Another guy rolled a trio but the last guy rolled four sixes. As he picked up the pot and was getting ready for the next round a thin dark haired man came and spoke something into his ear. They quickly paid their tab and left. A few minutes later a group of men in civilian clothes with badges hanging down their neck entered the bar and looked around. One of them went over to a corner and talked to Gigi who I saw shaking her head. She then came behind the bar and in paper cups poured some drinks and gave them to the men. They quickly drank it and left.

At this Bolin said, “Those men are from vice squad. They must be on the hunt for someone and that is why those guys that were rolling the dice left so quickly”.

We talked for a while and I told him I would get in touch.

I left the Torreon and was walking to my car. At about half a block I noticed a car was following me. All of a sudden a voice called out “Hey, are you all right? Do you need a ride, Rob?”

I turned and saw David Gonzalez driving down. I said “No thanks, I am fine. My car is right down there”.

“I know that”, David said. “I would like to invite you to lunch tomorrow. I really need to talk with you. How is 12:30 at La Mayorquina restaurant”?

“Sounds good to me but let me check my schedule. If there is any problem, I will call you”, I said

“Thanks see you at lunch”. David said and drove away.

Chapter 8

The party was going strong with a group of officials, partners and friends. It was being held at the penthouse of the Assistant Secretary of the Treasury in charge of operations, Manuel Rivera. It was in a very exclusive high rise in Santurce with a great view overlooking Laguna Los Corozos and Punta Las Marias Bay. The penthouse had three large bedrooms with high-end furniture. The master bedroom also had a study. There was a luxurious bathroom in each bedroom with double sinks, a bidet, a sunken tub and a separate shower and a big linen closet. The living room was well decorated with contemporary paintings and local artesan carvings. The dining room table could easily sit 14 persons. Rivera was middle-aged, short, and chubby, with a mustache and balding on the crown of his head.

In the study, Manuel Rivera was talking to the Assistant District Attorney from Ponce Candido Santin. Santin had just given him a briefing of the acquittals of some drug cases on the grounds of lack of evidence. Santin was tall and slender, with blond hair and dark eyes.

"It looks like the person bringing in the stuff (cocaine) is getting careless. They were lucky that the police were sloppy in this case. Nevertheless, most of the entire cargo was lost", Santin said.

"Well, I guess we have to tighten the screws on our folks. I will make a call. By the way, Lt. David Gonzalez has been snooping around. I thought he was supposed to be just in the metro area. He either knows too much or thinks he does. We don't need loose cannons out there", Rivera said.

"Don't worry about him. I'll have a talk with the Assistant Superintendent, Col. Maldonado, and ask him to task David on something in the metro area to keep him out of the south. Have you heard anything from the folks in Cartagena (Colombia)?" Santin asked.

"Nothing yet, but our man will soon have his boat out in the ocean on another pleasure trip. He was making some major repairs", Rivera answered.

There were people going in to the bathrooms where there were lines of cocaine and where they could take an undisturbed snort.

"What is Senator Lopez doing here? Santin asked.

"Hell, I had to invite him because he is the president of a commission I have to deal with. I know you are going to say he is an arrogant son of a bitch", Rivera said.

"I see you invited Senator Mendez and her partner Helena", Santin said.

(*It was known that Senator Mendez was a lesbian and Helena was her partner)*

"Yes, and by the way, I don't know if you heard that she and her partner are under investigation for all the traveling and unaccounted expenses", Rivera said.

"Uh oh, here comes Senator Valentine. I understand he is our competition. He goes to the Dominican Republic and brings a load of cocaine back in his yacht. The feds are keeping tabs on him so be careful", Santin said.

Rivera and Santin mingled among the crowd at the party shaking hands and talking to a few politicians. Two of them were members of the senate and one of the chambers. There was a District Court Judge and a Magistrate among the people that were users.

The Assistant Secretary of State was talking with the governor's aid when Santin came over and motioned to him to wipe his nose. The Asst. Secretary pulled out his handkerchief and made like he was sneezing so he wiped the left over cocaine off.

Chapter 9

Lt. David Gonzalez reported to the Police Department Headquarters in Rio Piedras at 9:00 AM at the request of the Assistant Superintendent, Colonel Maldonado. His office was on the third floor. David extended the usual formal courtesies as he entered the office.

"Good to see you David. How have you been?" Maldonado asked.

"I am fine, but really busy, thank you sir", David answered. "I understand you guys were at the Mar y Sol festivities and that resulted in quite a bust. Want to tell me about it?" Maldonado asked.

"Yes sir, I sent the superintendent a report. We had everything from cocaine, marijuana, firearms, and even liquor sales without the proper tax. The confiscated liquor was packed up and sent to the Revenue Agents", David said.

"Good job. Please take a look at this information here about a drug distribution point in La Perla where there is some unrest recently. There was a shootout and in the crossfire an 11 year old child was hit by a 9mm bullet. I really need you guys to investigate this turf war", Maldonado said.

"We are working on a tip from local residents in the area of Salinas regarding the drop off of a large quantity of marijuana and cocaine. We are starting surveillance and we really want to work this one out", David said.

"Well, send me the details on that task today so I can give it to the Ponce office. I need to give them something to do. I need you guys to work this La Perla thing out", Maldonado said.

"Shouldn't that be done by homicide squad?" David asked.

"The homicide squad is taking care of the investigation of the shooting of the child," Maldonado said.

David responded, "We are still gathering evidence and planning an undercover operation in Salinas".

"Well, put it all together. I'll have the Ponce office put someone on the case. I am sure they will follow all your recommendations", Maldonado said.

"OK, you will have the report by this afternoon", David said.

"David, I know your team is doing a great job out there and taking a lot of risks. Keep it up, you have a great future here", Maldonado said.

"Thank you sir", David said and left.

David rode back to his office cursing the moment he had stepped into the Colonel's office. David met with Maranda, Hector, Victor, Fernando and said "They are pulling us off the Salinas case. Let's wrap everything up and send it to them but keep your eyes and ears open".

Chapter 10

It was 12:35 P.M. when David arrived at La Mayorquina restaurant. Just as he entered and requested a table, I was also arriving. We were escorted to the rear of the restaurant where we sat in a quiet corner.

The waiter came to take our order. David had a local Corona beer and I ordered a gin and tonic.

"How is everything going?" David asked.

"Everything is going remarkably well. How have you been"? I asked.

"I think I've had better days. I got called to Headquarters by one of my many superiors and got assigned to work on some shooting at La Perla," David said.

We talked about the hot and humid weather. After noting the many traffic jams, we shifted onto local politics. These were tough years where the cultural identity of the Puertorrican was at stake. Having Fidel Castro win the revolution in Cuba had stirred up the pot here.

"There has been an increase in the activities of many organizations that are willing to use violence to change the status quo of the island. The Supreme Court of Puerto Rico has not been able to decide what the position of the island is or define what Estado Libre Associado (Free Associated State) means", David said.

"You know the history better than I do. I started out as a history major but I changed after a year with Professor Bonilla. I knew I was doomed," I said.

"I had Professor Bonilla and I could not stand the self-glorifying prick. The theory of one homogenous group under one flag did not work. You know why? It did not work and never will work because the Puertorricans want to keep their own identity". David said.

"One of the problems that we have", David continued, "is that teenagers going to New York and come back years later from Spanish Harlem thinking they are "made men." They want to take control of the drug distribution points", David said.

David knew Rob was articulate in this subject. He was an Army brat that grew up on the island. He studied in the University of Puerto Rico where he received his Bachelors in Social Science. He took R.O.T.C. and was a commissioned 2d Lieutenant. After training he was assigned to the 25th Infantry serving one tour in Nam. He got an honorable discharge and went to work with U.S. Customs. He later transferred to the Bureau of Narcotics. David knew all of this because he had done his homework. David remembered him from the UPR. David was a senior graduating in Political Science and received his officers' commission and was assigned to an artillery firebase near An Khe.

The waiter brought David a plate of "bacalao a la vizcaina" (cod in tomato stew over rice) and for Rob "arroz con gandures pernil" (rice with pigeon pees and roasted pork). They each ordered another drink.

David continued, "I don't know if your visits to the Torreon Bar were for social or business related reasons. But I want to give you some information. There are a group of individuals that meet frequently at that bar. They are from Argentina. They control most of the prostitutes that operate in the different bars. They also use them as mules to transport cash and drugs. These guys are international and when things get hot they hop on an airplane and skip town. The women work out of the Riviera Bar and the Black Angus Bar. Both have ties to the underworld syndicate in New York. The bars operate independently from these Argentinean thugs. In fact they are "persona non grata" there. I am just telling you this for your personal information, which you might already know. If I can be of assistance in any way, please let me know", David said.

I thanked David for his information and offer to help. "I will keep that in mind. I did see a couple of these guys in action at the Hilton Hotel. I didn't know at the time what was going on. I went to the Torreon out of curiosity and I saw the Argentinean crew there. When the Vice Squad came they were long gone", I said.

"They have paid informants and they know when it is safe to be in a location", David added. "Most of them have either expired visas or forged documents. The ones with good visas move frequently to keep in good standing with INS (Immigration Service). When the Argentineans come back from abroad, they send their women first with the narco packages. When the men arrive, they collect the drugs and make their transactions. That is the way the business goes."

My beeper went off and I excused myself and went to the telephone. I called the office and Don called me back to the office. I went to the table and told David I had to leave. I offered to pay the bill but David insisted it was his treat.

"We must continue this conversation at another time. I would like to talk a little bit about the social problems of this island", I said.

David answered, "Anytime."

I thanked David for the treat and said that the next one was on me.

Chapter 11

We met in Don's office and he said "We have some field work to do this afternoon. Joe has been working with a CI that has produced some information that might help us out. I will let Joe explain".

Joe told us, "Mingo, my CI (confidential informant), likes to gamble. He plays poker frequently and meets all sorts of people. He has been working on this man that he met in a card game. The man was flashing quite a bit of money. Mingo won a couple of big hands and the man started talking to him on his break from the game. He pulled out some cocaine and snorted it and asked Mingo if he wanted some. Mingo accepted the offer and took a snort. They then sat back down and continued in the card game. Mingo ran out of luck and had to leave. Two days later he met with this man again in a bar in the Condado. The man's name is Ricardo. Some of his friends at the bar called him "Ricardito" because he was a small guy. They had some drinks and planned to meet again for another game. I gave Mingo some cash and he went to the next game and his new best friend was there. After the game, at which Mingo did very well, Mingo invited him for a drink. They went out and partied for awhile. Mingo asked Ricardito for some cocaine to resell. At first Ricardito said that he was not a salesman just a user. Mingo pressed on the issue and he finally agreed to meet and arrange for a sale." Joe indicated that the meeting had been planned and that finally Ricardito had agreed.

"The meeting is going to be held in Restaurante La Costa over in Isla Verde. Ricardito selected the location. I checked out the area and the layout of the restaurant is an "L" shape with a main front door and rear emergency door. There is also a door out of the kitchen. This door leads out to the garbage cans. You can also circle around to the parking lot. The meeting is going to be held at 6:30PM. Mingo is carrying $2,000 cash to purchase a sample. Mingo will be wearing a wire. Andrew, you will be in the restaurant before Mingo arrives. Rob, I need you in the van with the recording device and the camera. I will be out on the street watching the entrance."

At 5:15 we were all in place casually observing and trying to be out of sight. Traffic was normal and just a few persons entered the restaurant. I was parked one block away within perfect view of the entrance and with clear audio. I thought about the conversation I had with David about the chaotic situation on the Island. I realized that I had showed a degree of ignorance when I knew better. After studying history and reading the newspapers, I knew that David had been right. There were people willing to go the extra mile to get the Island's independence.

Andrew was already in the restaurant and was eating some "arroz con huelles" (crabmeat over rice). He had changed his seat and when the waiter asked him why, he said that the air-conditioning was blowing on him and cooling off his meal. The seat he had now actually had a better view of the restaurant.

Joe was two blocks away in his car where he could quickly follow Mingo if needed.

At 6:25 pm Mingo came walking up the sidewalk. He had parked a block away. Mingo was about 5'7", 160 pounds, with tanned skin and dark long hair. His brown eyes scanned the area over and over. With his crooked nose he looked more Jewish than Puerto Rican. He had been busted for possession with intent to sell hash and heroin. He had served three years in a federal pen before he was paroled. That is why we recruited him to help us out. He stood in front of the restaurant and was looking around again as if searching for someone that could be following him. Just as he was going to enter, a man in a red Toyota corolla was slowly driving by looking towards the restaurant.

I took a picture of the red car. Mingo entered the restaurant and walked in the back where Ricardito and two other guys were sitting.

"How are you today Manny? Why don't you sit down and have a drink?" Ricardito asked. Mingo was using Manny as his cover.

"I am fine, thank you. I'll have a beer", Mingo responded.

They talked about football and then basketball. Mingo asked Ricardito about the drugs. He ignored the question and indicated they would talk about that later.

While they were talking, Andrew was still eating and had them in clear sight. All of a sudden, all four men got up and walked to the front door. They walked near Andrew as they talked about a poker game.

Out on the street, they turned right towards the parking lot. They all got into a blue Ford Taurus. Andrew walked out, slowly shaking his head. He knew we were going to tail Mingo and his friends.

I had snapped some pictures as they came out of the restaurant. I recognized two of the men that were with Mingo. I called Joe and told him to be looking out for the blue Ford Taurus that was heading in his direction. We all jumped into our vehicles and started to follow at a distance.

Chapter 12

Ricardito, Tony and Mingo drove in a circle looking for a tail. Mingo was wearing a wire so we could record the conversations for evidence. The streets were crowded. Mingo's conversation described the traffic and we discerned which direction they were going. They made several turns and ended up on Duffant Street and parked. They went up to the second floor of a four story building.

Mingo had talked during the trip and the conversation was all about a poker game they were going to have. Mingo mentioned again the drugs and Tony said they would get the delivery at the poker game.

In the apartment there were other men waiting to play. Mingo joked around a little as he acknowledged other people that were present. As he spoke to them, I noticed Mingo was nervous.

Joe, who was Mingo's handler, wasn't happy that they were not able to keep Mingo in sight. Mingo's wire was working well in the apartment. I heard them dragging something across the floor, possibly some furniture. Then I heard the shuffling of cards and the pot started at $25 each. As the game was played the only mention about cocaine was the invitation to snort.

It was past midnight and Mingo was ahead. One of the guys was getting a little itchy because he was loosing quite a bit. It sounded like the drugs and booze were catching up with him.

At about 3:00 AM I heard a knock on the door. Then, a greeting was heard, "Hola Charlie" and Charlie came in.

Then I heard Charlie say, "Ricardito, I'm in a hurry".

That was the signal and someone excused themselves from the game and it came to a halt. I heard them call Manny and they went to another room.

Ricardito said, "This is a contact of a contact. Do you have the money"?

Mingo said "I have a grand".

The contact then said "Its two grand".

Then Mingo said, "Just give me half then."

The contact said, "How in the hell do you expect me to cut and repack here. There is no deal. I came for two grand and that is what I am going out with".

Mingo then said "Listen, no need to get excited. I'll give you $1,700 and send the other $300 with Ricardito after the game".

Ricardito then said, "I will vouch for him".

The contact told Mingo, "OK, could you excuse us we need to talk".

Mingo then asked "Do we have a deal"?

The contact answered, "Hey man, I said I need to talk to Ricardito in private".

Mingo went back watch the card game. He no longer had the money to play with. The contact came out and asked Mingo to follow him to get the drugs. It sounded like they were climbing stairs. We heard him unlock a door and ask Mingo to sit down.

Ricardito and friends left the building after Mingo had gone upstairs. I had a hunch things were not going well. Shortly after, Mingo came out the front door. He stepped to the curb and looked both ways before crossing. He walked to the corner and hailed a taxi. He went back to the restaurant to get his car. He drove off to the rendezvous' point to meet Joe. He gave the small bag of cocaine to Joe. Joe tested it and it was high grade positive.

Mingo said, "The arrangement is to wait for a call from the contact. If there was no problem, the supplier would have 10 kilos ready. The money would have to be wired in advance to the bank the contact provides when he calls".

The name of the supplier, by what he saw on a tag of a gym bag, was Charles Maier.

"The supplier is white, about 5'10", with blond hair and green eyes. He was wearing blue jeans, sneakers, and a Grateful Dead t-shirt" Mingo said.

Joe gave me a call and passed the information on that Mingo had given him. I was a block away from the apartment house. I was observing the cars and the people in the area. Most of the people were dark skinned with dark hair and shorter than the description. About three hours later, I saw a tall, blond guy get into a BMW car parked down the street. He did not have a Grateful Dead t shirt on. He was dressed casually with dark slacks and a grey long sleeved shirt. I had a hunch he fit the description so I decided to follow him. The car traveled slowly, making quick turns and ended in Rio Piedras parking next to a red Toyota Corolla. He got into the Toyota and they took a spin around the corner. I stayed put and called it in.

An hour later the red Toyota came back and dropped him off. He drove off but the red Toyota stayed put. Joe called and told me to follow the BMW. Joe was about a block away and was going to follow the red Toyota.

I followed the BMW to Park Boulevard. He parked in front of a high rise and went in the main entrance. It was an apartment building facing the ocean. I could see his car from a block away, so I waited until a surveillance team arrived. Then I left.

CHAPTER 13

Don Manolo Rodriguez Inchautegui was resting in his villa, called "Pinos Calzos" in the outskirts of Cali, Colombia. The road to the villa was over a mile long surrounded by tall trees. There was a gate house staffed by security guards at the end of the road. About 100 yards further, there were the guest quarters. The guest quarters were connected by a covered walk leading to the main house. Don Manolo was short, portly, and always elegantly dressed. He was a serious gentleman very well known and highly respected in political circles. He inherited over 2000 acres of land and was farming bananas, coffee and other small fruits. He recently ventured into the fresh flower business specializing in orchids. He had two sons Calixto and Jose. Calixto, known as Atisbador, (*the snooper)* was the eldest and held more responsibilities in the business. Jose Antonio, known as Ingenioso (*the ingenious)* was well educated and spoke Spanish, English and French. He was the customer service rep for the business and travelled to many different countries.

There were over 1000 acres of coca in addition to what was planted beneath the coffee and banana trees. Calixto took care of having a crew pick the coca and get it refined. At one time, he was shipping coca to a processing plant in Ecuador. Now he had his own refinery in the jungles near Pasto, Colombia. He had several well paid hench men that worked for him. One of these men, Severiano Hernandez, along with two others, Jacinto Rivera and Pablo Escobedo, travelled to different countries to deliver the final product of cut cocaine.

Calixto came into Don Manolo's study and said, "We sent another shipment to Haiti yesterday. From there, the cocaine will be shipped to the buyers in Puerto Rico and Miami. Pablo will pick up the money in Haiti. Severiano, our point man in Puerto Rico, will pick up the cash there. From Miami, Rodolfo will stop in Puerto Rico and pick up all the money from Severiano."

"Have proper transportation arrangements been made for Rodolfo and Pablo?" Don Manolo asked.

"Yes, Rodolfo is going by boat to the Dominican Republic. There he will meet with Pablo and a charter flight will bring them directly to us", Calixto said.

"I understand that there might be a little trouble in Jalisco, Mexico. It looks like there is a turf war going on", Calixto mentioned.

"Yes I've heard about that. We don't want to get involved in that", Don Manolo said. "Let them settle their own fights and we'll deal with whoever is left".

"What about the vegetables and coffee that we sent to Spain?" Don Manolo asked.

Calixto indicated they were on schedule. "The ship left Barranquilla and should be there by the end of the week."

"I just got a load of orchids, mostly catleya and phalenopsis", Don Manolo said. "I need to send them to customers in Ponce, Puerto Rico, Tampa, Florida, and Paterson, New Jersey. They must go air freight", Don Manolo said.

"I need the paperwork to make the air transport arrangements." Calixto said.

"What's the status on the playground we are building in El Arenal?" Don Manolo asked. *(El Arenal is a small town near Pinos Calzos)*

"The equipment came in and has been installed. We added an obstacle course. The city gave us an adjacent field and we built two soccer fields", Calixto said.

"I am glad. We must continue to help our surrounding communities", Don Manolo said and left the room.

Chapter 14

It was early Friday morning. I had just taken a shower, when I got a call from Andrew.

"Hey Rob, we need you over at the office right now", Andrew said.

I didn't ask questions. I just said "be right there".

When I arrived, I went directly to the conference room adjacent to Don's office.

"It looks like we are all here. Joe is on his way. Joe's operation with one of his CI's has been compromised", Don said.

At that same moment, Joe entered the room.

Don said "Let me turn it over to Joe. He can brief us on what happened".

Joe said, "The local Police Narcotics gave me call. It seems that this morning at about 5:30 a.m., a man was driving up Rt. 191, El Yunque, when he saw a body on the side of the intersection of 9938. When he checked the body, the person was already dead. He went to the nearest telephone and called the Police. The body was Mingo's. He was tortured, throat slit, tongue was cut out and laid on top of a sign on his chest. The sign read "El chota, meaning the rat.

"Oh shit! Oh shit!" I said.

"What's the matter, Rob?" Joe asked.

"It brings back memories. We lost three advisers in Nam. When we finally found them their throats were slit, skin peeled off and they had several bullet holes", I said.

"Sorry about that. If it is too much for you just wait outside", Don said.

"Oh, I can take it. It was just a flashback. Do we have confirmation that it was Mingo?" I asked.

"Yea, I drove up and saw the body myself. I asked the Police for pictures and prints", Joe said.

Don said, "Someone must have been following him very closely. But, let's wait for confirmation before we jump to any conclusions."

"I think we ought to go after Charles who sold Mingo the dust and that I had followed", I said.

"It will be better to wait for more information before we go out on our own. Besides, this is a homicide and it will be investigated by the local Police. We don't want to get in their way. So, let's just keep our eyes and ears open and be careful", Don said.

Joe indicated that he had a confidential source that was going to provide more information. Joe said he would keep us posted. After everyone left, Joe approached Don and said, "I am afraid that Rob is going to go searching for this guy, Charlie. If he finds him, he might just go ballistic. You know what he did in Atlantic City and NYC"?

"OK, I know." Don said, "Let's not jump to conclusions".

I went back to my desk and read the briefing reports Don had given me. I read about the area of Humacao, a town on the eastern side of the island where a local drug bust had gone sour. The dealers managed to leave the scene with the drugs. The same thing had happened in Salinas twice. Salinas was a town on the southern part of the island, near Ponce. Salinas was known for its beaches and good fish. I started thinking this might be an inside job. In "La Perla", there was a shootout with three casualties. La Perla was a neighborhood near the El Morro castle area in Old San Juan. It borders on the rocky coast of the Atlantic Ocean.

Because of its secluded location, it's attractive to drug dealers and arms smugglers. It was a very dangerous area where even the police would tread carefully. The casualties at La Perla were not all local residents. They might have been trying to invade the sacred turf of La Perla.

"This whole thing about Mingo's death doesn't look right" I thought to myself. "There had to be someone at the restaurant that saw Mingo and I think it was the guy in the red car. Then I got a call.

Chapter 15

I got a call from David, the one person I was thinking about calling.

"Hey, we need to have a little social. Could you meet with me in about an hour for cocktails"? David asked.

"As long as you pay, I will go anywhere", I said.

"Good, meet me in Rio Piedras at the Monos Bar. Do you know where that is?" David said.

"Yes, I think it's over by the University", I said.

"Yes, on Madrid Street. You might have to walk a little because parking is not good", David said.

"Not to worry. I can manage", I responded.

"See you", David said and the line went dead.

I went downstairs and got in my car. I knew it would take me a while. A few police cars passed me going toward Rio Piedras. They were parking at the entrance of the university. The students were up to something. It brought back memories of when FUPI (*Future University Pro Independence)* would barricade the entrance to the university and provoke riots.

I arrived at "El Mono" bar and entered. I saw a couple of men staring at me. One of them came up to me and said "Hi cutie, would you like to have a drink with me?"

"Hey, come over here", David said.

Two of the men started singing out "Pato patito pato patuleco".

"Glad you saved me from that one. I see this is a Gay bar. Why on earth are we meeting here?" I asked.

"Yes it's the safest place to talk about history", he said. The waiter came over and asked us what we wanted. We ordered our drinks. The waiter stood nearby listening to what we were talking about.

Then, David said, "On July 25 1898, the Americans invaded the island through the town of Guanica. Ever since then we have had people demonstrate their displeasure toward the United States".

"I had to come in here just in case I was followed. Nobody would suspect I was having a meeting here with a Federal Agent", David said.

"I studied the history and know it well. So you don't have to give me history lessons. And by the way, on that same date, General Nelson Mile led the troops into Guanica. It was President McKinley who took Puerto Rico as a "bounty of war". Do you think someone is eyeing you?" I asked.

"Well, for starters" David said, (ignoring my question) "they changed the name from Puerto to Porto, good thing it was never accepted. They considered that this was an island full of Indians and slaves and they did not know what to do with us".

David and Robin continued with their history debate waiting for the crowd to take their eyes and ears off of them.

David looked around and said "Sorry, about that guy found in El Yunke".

"What do you know about that"? I asked.

"Rumor has it, that there were Colombians mixed up with a bad ass cop. They did a number on him and are long gone. Another rumor is that there is a death squad controlled by a Colonel in the police. They were the ones who murdered the son of the president of the independence party. If this be the case, the higher ups and their cohorts are getting a piece of the pie", David said.

(*We were being watched again).*

"I see your knowledge of history is good. It was President Truman who said that the people on the island were able to decide for themselves whether they wanted a democratic government or not. Only then, would Congress consider changing the political status of the island. There would then be a need for a plebiscite. Congress had already eliminated the statehood option. President Truman vetoed the bill presented in Congress for a plebiscite. He thought that the people of Puerto Rico should decide their future and not Congress", I said.

David said, "The entire situation of the island could have been solved in the elections of 1944. Munoz Marin should have kept his mouth shut. People would have voted for the independence. Munoz had a platform built on "The status is not an issue". To refocus the people away from independence, he promised a plebiscite as soon as the elections were over".

I wanted to ask David about Maranda. I really didn't know his status or how he would interpret it. I decided this was not the right time.

The waiter had left and the people around us weren't listening anymore.

David said, "Your knowledge of history is very good. It's as solid as my source. There is a group of higher ups that know your movements".

"I think I know who they are", I said. We finished our second drink and I got up to leave. David said, "Wait, let's go out the back door. It's safe and the alley leads to the street".

As I followed David, he told the owner we were leaving out the back door. He gave the waiter a $20 and told him to keep the change. The waiter almost kissed him. When we were outside I said, "Let me know if he got anymore information".

David said, "We will meet again soon". He disappeared before I could say anything else.

CHAPTER 16

"The Puerto Rican Nationalist Party was founded in response to the invasion by the U.S. In 1924, Pedro Albizu Campos, a Harvard attorney was elected president of the party. During 1930 there was a report published by the Brookings Institute indicating that the Island was in a desperate crisis. Pedro Albizu Campos demonstrated that the report was full of errors. The capitalists controlled the agriculture, sugar and tobacco industries and had made a huge profit for themselves", Antulio Gomez said. He was explaining the history to his friends, Pedro Ocasio, Antonio Perez, Alejandro Ramirez and Manuel Ojeda all members of the "Macheteros ".

"I can talk about history and give you all kinds of pep talks but we won't get anything done just by talking. We have been promised some C4 (semtex explosives) in exchange for but another drug delivery. Pedro, we are going to need your boat. The pick-up is between the islands of Vieques and Culebra. We will be meeting a fishing trawler. We have to bring the cargo to the Maunabo beach area where ground support will pick it up. We have to move fast to avoid the police. Once we deliver we will head on out, to Vieques and lay low", Antulio said.

Alejandro said, "I think it is too soon since we recently shot the Navy van over in Sabana Seca. We killed and wounded sailors and destroyed Navy property constituting a federal offense. All federal agents and local law enforcement will be after us. I think we should lie low".

Antulio responded, "I understand your concern. Look at it this way, everything we did was inland so they will be looking for us inland. We ship out, spend some time at sea and then things will have cooled off. We will pick up make our delivery, then go back out and fish on our way in".

"Well, it's a plan. Let's just hope the trawler is on time and most of all that ground support for the delivery is there", Pedro said.

Five days later they were at sea in Pedro's 35 foot Chris Craft equipped with twin 400 hp engines. After a day at sea, in the middle of the night they caught up to the trawler. They loaded 10 packages containing 20 kilos of cocaine each from the trawler.

It took them two days to reach the coast of Maunabo. The ground crew came out in a skiff and took the cocaine. They dropped off 2 five pound bags of plastic explosives and the detonators.

On their way to Vieques, Pedro's boat was flagged down by the U.S. Coast Guard. They made a cursory inspection and waved them off. Lucky for them they had their fishing gear displayed. They stopped in Vieques and spent a couple of days walking around. After that they refueled and set sail back to Humacao.

Chapter 17

I got to the office early in the morning with the intention of doing some research. I searched several connections to the traffic between the islands and the major players. As I settled in with coffee, I picked up some papers from reports, newspaper articles and notes. Lidia then called asking if I had seen today's San Juan Star. A featured article in the newspaper explained in detail that the police narcotic division had made a raid in Bayamon. They had found firearms, 3 kilos of cocaine and 100 cannabis bricks in a house. The other headline story was about a shooting at Isla Verde Restaurant. Yuyo, the boss of the Lloren Torres drug point, and two of his men were having dinner with Turin. Turin was the boss of the Campo Rico drug point. When Yuyo got up and went to the bathroom his gunman shot Turin twice in the head. Yuyo and his gang now run Campo Rico. The last article in the newspaper was about a bomb that had exploded in Mayaguez square killing two prominent members of the independence party. It led me to the conclusion that there was a death squad.

After reading the newspaper, I got involved in my work when Lidia called and said, "You have a call ".

I asked her, "Who was it?"

She said, "Codename history buff".

I said, "I'll take it".

David said," Hey, buddy. I have something interesting that I think you should come and see. Go over to Isla Grande air field and ask for Galo. He is a Major in the Ntl. Guard and will fly you here in his helicopter. There is some heavy drug business on the west coast of the island I would like you to see."

"Okay, I 'm on my way".

I checked out of the office and went to Isla Grande (a Navy base many years ago that was converted into a government office center). I found Galo who was waiting for me over by the airfield. I flew in the co-pilot seat of a HU1 which brought me back to the Vietnam era.

David was waiting for me at the main terminal of Ramey AF base. The base had been part of the Strategic Air Command, housing the B-52's and KC-135's up until 1970 when it was changed to a local airport because it no longer was of strategic value.

"This better be good," I said.

We drove off and David said, "We are going to the hospital to interview a man that was knifed".

I said "OK. I will be all ears".

We went to Aguadilla to the hospital and they allowed us to visit Mr. Roul Felicino. Roul with Mr. Uto River were owners of a business called "Eight Ball Bar" located on Marina Street in downtown Aguadilla.

"Mr. Felicino, could you tell us what happened to you? David asked.

Mr. Felicino said, "I own a bar on Marina St. and we close late at night. I usually do the locking up. On several occasions I noticed a boat signaling with flashing lights toward the shore. I was curious and saw that it was once a week that the signaling went on. I got my binoculars out and looked out at a Cruise ship. I also saw a motor boat leaving the area where the ship was. The night I got stabbed, there was a full moon. I was across the street when I realized the motor boat was picking up packages. A man came up behind me and stabbed me in my side. When I turned to look at him, he stabbed me again. He took off running away when two people saw me fall and came to rescue me. They brought me to the emergency room".

"What kind of packages were they?" I asked.

"The packages were floating because they were pulling them out of the water. They were about 20 to 30 inches long and about 15 or 20 inches tall. I couldn't see how wide they were," Mr. Felicino said.

After we got all the information from Mr. Felicino we went down to the police station on the outskirts of the town of Aguadilla. The officer in charge of narcotics showed us evidence obtained from a fisherman who had picked up one of the floating packages. It was a neat 20 by 20 inch inflatable containing cannabis bricks. The marking on the bricks were from the Mexican Gulf organization which meant they were branching out. The officer in charge of narcotics told us it was not the first time reports like this had come in. He never had the evidence picked up by a local fisherman. The officer said he alerted the marine police in Mayaguez. The cruises were now in season and it would be difficult to trail behind them since there is one every other day.

I called the office and notified Don on what was going on in the area.

David said, "I must stop at a bar at the entrance of town in the area called El Mondongo and talk to the Machimbo brothers. They control the illegal lottery and other activities in this area. If I am not back in 15 minutes go to the police station and bring them over".

Ten minutes later David came back.

"The brothers say to talk to Lord Carson. He controls the upper beach and Ramey area up to Jobos Beach in Isabella. He is a short guy with a full head of black dyed hair and a thin mustache." David said.

David was giving me a lift back to San Juan. We decided to stop at a bar just before the Guajataka hill. The bar was called La Revancha and owned by a gambler named Kino El Tuerto because he had a glass eye. He was running a dice game in the back room.

To get to the bar you had to drive up a semi-paved hill where the lookouts could identify any cop vehicles approaching. We were in a blue mustang so the lookout wasn't alerted.

David said, "Let me go in and talk to Carson. I know Kino and I had a conversation with Carson once, so let's see what I can find out".

David went in to speak to Lord Carson. I stayed in the car. Twenty minutes later David came out.

"I got him on a winning streak and he was taking a break to piss. He said he does not deal with drugs but heard that there is some drug dumping over by Desecheo Island. This Island is over by the Rincon point so the drugs must be entering there. The Island is deserted which means that someone can stash stuff there and pick it up when the sea is calm. It is in the area of the Mona Passage. Carson doesn't know who the people are. If he finds out anything, he will let me know", David said.

We drove off to San Juan. David invited me to his home.

When we arrived at his home David said, "This is my wife Zulma". Then he started introducing me to the rest of the family.

Zulma is a Teacher at Junior High", David said.

Zulma was a very nice looking young lady. He continued with the introductions, his sister-in-law Marisel and his mother-in-law Aida.

"This is Zulma Iris, my oldest daughter. She is in fourth grade. All "A's", and this little one is Carico. She is in first grade", David proudly said.

We had a great meal. I enjoyed the home cooking very much.

"Let's go to the terrace in the back where we can enjoy these panatelas (Cuban cigars) and some brandy", David said.

We sat enjoying our smoke and slowly savoring our brandy.

"You have a beautiful family and a very comfortable home", I said.

"Thanks . . . I appreciate it. (He served another brandy). It gives me pleasure to serve you as my guest and I appreciate what you are doing for my country. We need to get rid of the scum that is bringing the rotten stuff into the lives of my people", David said

After a moment of silence I asked, "Is Maranda married?"

"No. Why do you ask?" David asked.

"No specific reason, David", I said

"She was engaged once and the jerk was fooling around and she caught him. That was the end of the engagement and almost the end of the jerk. She beat the shit out of him. She is a good girl, Rob. I wouldn't want to see her hurt", David said.

"I understand, David. Thanks", I said.

"You know she has a masters in psychology. I don't know why she doesn't leave the force and go work on her own", David said.

I finished my second brandy and half of my cigar and said goodbye, thanking everyone even the two little girls who came to wish me a good night.

CHAPTER 18

Don Manolo Rodriguez flew directly to Madrid, Spain. At Barajas International airport he was met by the commercial attaché of the Colombian Embassy who helped with his luggage and drove him back to his apartment. On the way he was briefing Don Manolo on the economy in Spain. Spain at the time was going through a transformation crisis which had the economy on a rollercoaster. They arrived at the pent house located on Avenida Padre Huidobro overlooking Casa de Campo Park. That evening Don Manolo had invited the Spanish Minister of Finance and Economy, Don Vicente Lopez de Haro for diner.

"Don Vicente, how nice of you to have dinner with me", Don Manolo said.

"It's always a pleasure to dine with you and have the opportunity to chat about current affairs in America", Don Vicente said. "And by the way, I want to thank you for your generosity of your gift. The coffee is well savored and the orchids are added a touch of fresh air and a sparkle of light to our offices".

"Well, Don Vicente, I have branched out into our own grown orchids and have also managed to harvest an extensive collection of wild orchids. My plan is not to abandon the other business but to improve on something that is in line with my hobby. I have a farm house and several hundred acres in San Jose de Guavire where we are cultivating my orchids and flowers. The staff there is very knowledgeable and takes good care of the property. We pick the flowers and prep the orchids then bring them to Bogota for export", Don Manolo said.

"So, that sounds good, what is going to happen to your other farm, Pinos Calzos"? Don Vicente asked.

"I will be leaving it to my son Calixto. I want Jose to do the travel back and forth for me. In the meantime I will stay in Madrid where I am opening two businesses. One is at Arturo Soria Plaza. It will be an exclusive flower and coffee shop. The other is at Moda Shopping over at Paseo La Castellana", Don Manolo said.

They continued their chat while having dinner.

The next day Don Manolo met with the Vice President of Banca Iberica where he went over several accounts. Later his attorney and the banks attorney met to consolidate the purchase of the two store locations. The ownership of the stores was registered in two corporations keeping them separate from the business in Colombia.

The following week Don Manolo hosted a reception at Arturo Soria Plaza. Among the guest were financial investors, bankers, government ministers, and the Police Commissioner. The event was catered by an exclusive service and there was a constant flow of champagne and Spanish wines.

Don Manolo called Jose Antonio to give him the good news about the successful grand opening.

"It went very well and I was talking with the Chief of Staff of the Prime Minister who wants us to invest in an apartment building. A contractor started it and he defaulted so the government had to take it over", Don Manolo said.

"Sounds like a good way to invest some of our surplus. On another subject, the Mexican governments have started cracking down on marijuana production which will shift the market toward our area", Jose Antonio said.

"I would suggest we share that part of the market with Medellin. Let them have most of the operation and we can concentrate on the cocaine", Don Manolo said.

"I think it is a good idea and I will meet with Carlos in Medellin", Jose Antonio said.

"I will be around here for a while so if you need me just call", Don Manolo said and hung up.

CHAPTER 19

Three days had gone by and I was in the office reviewing some intell reports. I went over the local items from the night before. It was the usual, one death in La Perla and another in Puerta de Tierra. At a public housing development, San Jose in Rio Piedras, the police arrested Pizarro Colon alias "Wily", and seized cocaine, marijuana and $2,500. In Santurce, Pablo Marrero was arrested with a half kilo of cocaine, $7,500 and two firearms. In Sabana Gardens, Carolina Jose Sanjurjo, the drug contact there, was arrested and one kilo of cocaine and $11,000 seized. In Bayamon Gardens Ariel Lance was arrested with heroin, cocaine and $5,000 seized.

I decided to go talk to Don about something I had in mind. I was waved into his office by his secretary.

"I was thinking of contacting this Charles Maior to arrange a purchase", I said.

"How are you going to work it out?" Don asked.

"Well I was going to use the sample that Mingo got from him. I will work on the assumption that Mingo was legit and that his sample was good", I said.

"That's not a good idea. You need something other than Mingo's purchase. Remember Mingo is dead because they had branded him as an informer" Don said.

After discussing other alternatives I went back to my desk.

The telephone rang and I picked up. It was David.

'Were you at the airport last night"? David asked.

"No, I wasn't. I heard this morning that there were some explosions" I said.

"The Macheteros blew up 8 air national guard jets", David said.

"How do you know it was the Macheteros?" I asked.

"Because they left their calling card, an 18 inch machete and a red flag with a black star in the middle".

"Was anyone hurt?" I asked.

"No, it was just directed at the aircraft", David said.

"Was there any type of security there"? I asked.

"Yes, they had some rent-a-cops, but it could have been none at all. Whoever it was they went in and out without being detected" he responded.

"What's the word out on the street?" I asked.

"Nothing yet, but I wonder where they got the explosives. It was military grade", David said.

I thanked him for the information and told him we should meet soon for a drink.

I went back to my morning reports. I was getting the picture. There was a turf war going on. Each public housing development had its own drug outfit. At times, they try to flex their muscles and take over part of their neighbor's territory.

Don came by and said "I checked on the cruise ships that had recently arrived in the port of San Juan. I found that Carnival and Norwegian were the only two. Holland America and Celebrity are scheduled to leave today. Royal Caribbean and Princess are due in tomorrow".

I thanked him for updating me with the cruise ship schedule.

He added "Carnival went to Aruba, Curacao, Jamaica, Cancun and back. Norwegian went to the Virgin Islands, Grenada, St.

Martin, Trinidad and back. Our best bet is to keep an eye on Carnival".

"I agree. We should find out when the next one is leaving".

"Carnival will sail tonight and they are following the same route. It's a 7 day cruise so they should be west of the Island in 6 days", Don said.

"I will contact the people in Mayaguez," I responded.

"Well, tell them to only observe at a distance. We really want to find out where their supply line is coming from. If what they are picking up is from the Gulf area it would mean Cancun. But what if they get their supply brought up to one of the Islands?" Don asked.

"I got it. I will talk to them and give them the information", I said.

I went out to Mayaguez and met with the area narcotic commander, the marine police commander. We agreed on how we would proceed. I told them I would try to be back in the area in 5 days.

CHAPTER 20

I had just come back from making inquiries on the process of bank licensing. The applications are submitted to the P.R. Treasury Department, bureau of licensing. Then an investigation is carried out. I managed to get some information from them on the Banco Real de Finanzas. On the record, the president and general manager was a Cuban born with American citizenship by the name of Antonio Chelles. The bank was a small one, located in Santurce on Condado Street. The building is made of concrete with a glass security entrance door. You had to be buzzed in by an armed security guard in order to enter.

I received a call from my contact in Miami. I had asked them to check for any records on Mr. Chelles, but they had found nothing.

My contact in INS (Immigration) faxed me some of the documentation submitted for the naturalization process of Mr. Chelles. I rode by the bank at different times. I saw a few of the same men that were in the Torreon Bar. They looked either Colombian or Argentinean. One of the men fit the description of Mr.Chelles, 5'7", weight around 154, and about 39 years old. His hair was dark, neatly cut and he wore a tailor made pinstripe dark suit.

I couldn't pinpoint their connection to the bank other than there was a money laundering operation going on. I got called into Don's office and I thought this would be a good opportunity to talk about this.

"The guy you wanted to interview, Maior, is dead", Don said.

"How did it happen?" I asked.

"Well, let me start with at the beginning. Early this morning, at 2:00am, Maior was traveling on Baldorioty de Castro. A witness said he had stopped at a traffic light. Just as he was going to move, two guys on a motorcycle emptied about 40 rounds of 9 mm, probably an UZI", Don said

"I guess he didn't have a chance", I said.

"No, someone was traveling not far behind in a red Toyota. He went in Maior's car pretending to check on him. He cleaned out the glove compartment and under the seat. Maior was transporting some white powder, cocaine", Don said.

"Did they find any weapons or money?" I asked.

"No, looks like the guy in the red Toyota did a good job cleaning up", Don said.

"Who is the guy in the red Toyota? I asked.

"We checked the license plates and they're stolen", Don said.

"Well, I think the next time we see the red Toyota we should just stop him", I said.

"I gave the information to the local authorities, but they haven't reported anything yet", Don said.

I changed the subject and told Don about the Banco Real and my suspicion about money laundering.

Don asked "What makes you think that's what's going on?. They may be just good friends and are going out for dinner".

"Well, you have a point there. This is just speculation and we will continue discreetly to find more evidence", I said and I left Don's office.

Chapter 21

I was summoned to federal court in Manhattan. The case involved three Mexicans running cocaine ring for the Sinaloa organization. It had been postponed several times due to the attorney's illness and later because of a death in the family. They had pleaded not guilty and that is why it was going to trial. The attorney was trying an entrapment defense.

I went directly to ADA Bobby Arnot who was the same prosecuting attorney I had for the casino case.

"Look I don't think we have to bring your informant to testify but I have his affidavit ready", Bobby said.

"The informant my partner and I met with these guys on three occasions. The first was just to establish and interest. On the second we displayed the money. On the third is when we make the buy bust", I said.

"Yes I got all that. These guys were able and willing?" Bobby asked.

"Yes, they were willing and they had the means and the opportunity", I said

So we went to trial and it lasted a week, ending with a verdict of guilty.

After the verdict we went to the Irish pub for some drinks.

At the pub I was informed by the Special Agent in Charge of the New York Office that I was to return to Washington HQ for a meeting.

I got on the early morning train and made it to DC. I went to the Director of Operations office and met with Col. Harrington. He was a cantankerous man who irritated me. With his soft verbose he could carry on and drive me nuts.

"I understand your casino case went well with the conviction of the Cubans", Col. Harrington said.

"Yes, we did have some hiccups along the way but we nailed them well", I said.

"Well Robin, you know the use of excessive lethal force not only is a hiccup for you but also for the agency. The director was not happy when he saw the injury report," He said.

I sat there fuming thinking why do I have to listen to this shit again.

"What about the three Mexicans?" He asked.

"They were all convicted. I think one of them is going to produce some intell for the New York Office. If they work him well", I said.

"Things seem to be getting out of hand in Puerto Rico. It's snowing in Puerto Rico so they say around here. I read that bullets are flying all over the place and people get killed every day with some collateral damage", he said.

"Well most of it is turf or territory invasion. In other words, shots are fired in the public housing because someone tries to take over the drug point. The end result is a confrontation where even children get hurt in the crossfire. The other thing is that the traffic in heroin has gone to its lowest while snow, cocaine, has doubled", I said.

"I don't know which is worst Puerto Rico or Mexico. Anyway, please give this bag to Don. Its stuff I did not want to send in the mail for him", He said.

"Will do sir", I answered.

I was glad to get out of his office. On my way out I was called by director of the intelligence desk Marty Diets.

"Robin, how is it going over in the Island of snow? He asked.

"We are having some progress", I said.

"Great. Listen, I have here some information that might be useful to you all. This lady, Geri Blanco it is thought she might be in P.R. You know who I am talking about right?" He asked.

"Yea, the black widow she was running the business up in Queens and we never could get a bead on her. I thought she was in Florida someplace", I said.

"Yes, she was running most of the business in south Florida but now we have reason to believe she is somewhere in your turf. Here is a copy of the indictment just in case you bump into her", Marty said.

"Well, thanks for the heads up", I said.

I walked out of the building as fast I could and got a cab to the airport. After I arrived at my apartment I took a shower got dressed and drove to San Juan. I went to my office, checked messages, shuffled some paperwork and left. I was walking to my car when I saw Maranda walking on the other side of the street. She looked very attractive with her short blue skirt and red blouse. There was something in the way she moved and how the wind played with her slightly wavy hair that made me cross the street and call her.

"Hi again", she said.

"I was just about to get something to eat would you like to join me", I said.

"I really don't know you. What did you say your name was?" she asked.

"Oh, how stupid can I be. I am Robin, Joe's partner. We met at Mar y Sol", I said.

"Yes but that does not mean that I am going to break bread with you. I am late to a previous engagement", She said.

"OK, I apologize. Can I invite you on another day when you have time?" I asked.

"I don't know. Let me think about it. See ya", she said.

"Ok, OK, Thanks", I said.

Chapter 22

Don Manolo came back to Bogota to and was on his way to his flower farm when Jose came by to talk to him.

"Two guys came over with Ms.Blanco and put in an order of 300kilos. I think the guys are from the CIA. We can get that amount right away from the FARC. (Armed Revolutionary Front of Colombia) The two guys said they would fly into one of our airstrips and pick up the load", Jose said.

"How are they paying for that?" Don Manolo asked.

"They are trading the drugs for weapons and ammunition", Jose said.

"What's the breakdown? Are they going to be able to cover the cost of production?" Don Manolo asked.

"It's going to be 400 AK-47 new and 120,000 rounds of ammunition", Jose said.

"That sounds reasonable if they bring all of it. Our production cost for this is $450,000 and the market value today is ten million. Did you find out where they are taking it to?" Don Manolo asked.

"No, but I guess part of it will go to Ms.Blanco and will end up in Miami and the CIA will use the rest to pay for their covert operations", Jose said.

"You see, if she distributes out to one or two suppliers she will net 2million and that way she just has one deal", Don Manolo said.

"If she gets greedy she will hold back and probably divide it between different suppliers netting a lot more profit", Jose said.

"Yes and risk getting caught which will not be good for us if she talks", Don Manolo said.

"The Americans have their eyes on her. There is no love between the CIA and the drug agency. If she gets caught they might try to extradite us", Jose said.

"Good thing extradition does not apply in Colombia. By the way I understand we finished construction of the annex to the Church of Nuestra Senora de la Candelaria. The Monsignor told me the new organ we ordered for them has arrived. I need you to swing by and make sure everything is fine Jose", Don Manolo said.

"I probably should try a more intimate approach with Ms. Blanco", Jose Antonio said.

"I don't think that is appropriate. This is strictly business. No hanky-panky. Ok", Don Manolo said.

"Yes, I will go to the church after I load the cargo for the CIA and Ms. Blanco", Jose said.

Two days later Jose and his men were at an old abandoned landing strip. The CIA guys' came back alone with pilots and a loadmaster in a C-130. The hatch was open and they came over to Jose and asked to see the drug.

"We brought our own test and weight equipment", one of the men said.

He started the test process while Jose's men counted the AK's and ammunition as they unloaded the aircraft.

"Take 10 cases of the AK and 10 cases of ammunition and put them on that truck and move it to Pinos Calzos to my storage", Jose said to one of his men.

After the aircraft left Jose made sure the rest of the AK and ammunition were neatly stored in the shed at the airstrip where members of the FARC would come and pick it up and then disappear.

Back at Pinos Calzos Jose checked his storage to make sure the weapons and ammunition was there then he went to talk to Don Manolo.

"So Ms. Blanco was not with the CIA guys when they picked up? Don Manolo asked.

"No she was not. I did not ask because I knew it was none of my business", Jose said.

"She is a sharp operator and I am sure she was not far away. By the way where is Calixto?" Don Manolo asked.

"He was at our north landing strip getting the airplane ready for Ginea Bissau with cargo that should go to Naples and Catania. The cargo we sent last week to Denmark and Hamburg arrived safely The money has been moved through several accounts and banks so it cannot be traced", Jose said.

"I will be going to San Jose Guavire to deal with the flowers. You know where to reach me if you need me. If I am not there I will probably be at the business in Madrid.

"I will let you know as soon as Calixto comes back".

Chapter 23

I was in the office sorting through some reports when I received a call from David.

"Listen, I got a call from Galo when he was at Isla Grande putting his helicopters to rest. He saw a stretch limo drive up on the tarmac. It stopped by a twin beach airplane. The driver, in uniform, got out to help the passengers and pulled out large suitcases. There were three women and two men in dark suits", David said.

"Hold on David", I said. "Why did Galo call you about this? Isn't it normal that people go to airports in limos and carry suitcases?"

"Well, he went over to the flight control office and their flight did not originate here. It came from St. Thomas earlier. They refueled and filed a flight plan back to St. Thomas", David said.

"O K, so it's not normal to get on a charter inbound flight?" I asked.

"No, what he explained is that it is not normal to bring an inbound flight to this area of the airport. Most flights go to the main terminal. The flight control officer said that one of the pilots had federal credentials, like CIA or FBI. Galo thought there was an awful lot of luggage for just a couple of nights to St. Thomas", David said.

"So, they went directly to the tarmac and boarded the airplane?" I asked.

"Yes, they didn't bother to stop by the terminal. I am at the airport right now picking up a copy of the flight plan. I'll see what else I can scoop up", David said.

I thanked him for the information and asked if he could fax me copies of what he picked up. I called a contact in St. Thomas and asked if they could verify incoming flight of any twin beach aircraft with five passengers three female and two male.

I went over to Don's office and briefed him on this information. "Look I know it might sound farfetched but it could be Ms. Blanco and her entourage. According to Marty Deets, she was somewhere around the Island", I said.

"It could be some congressman and friends on a hush, hush trip to the Island", Don said.

"O K let's see what information I can get", I said.

Three hours later I had a call from my contact in the St. Thomas area. He said there were no flights inbound like I had described. So I called Anguila and talked to one of the Constables. He had a direct contact with the airport and called me back to tell me there had been no aircraft landing as described. I also had called St. Martin and spoke to an Interpol representative there. I was just giving up when the Interpol representative from St. Martin called me back. He said they had no inbound flights as I had described coming in. But, he had alerted other Interpol agents. The one in Basse Terre, Guadeloupe had reported information of an inbound flight to Isla Aves which belong to Venezuela. Also, there had been a flight taking off from that Island and it was inbound to Colombia. I thanked them and went over to Don's office.

"Don the flight went from here to Isla Aves and from there they went to Colombia", I said.

"Let's alert some people in our embassy in Colombia and see what they come up with", Don Said.

"OK I will get on it", I said.

CHAPTER 24

David and his crew went to La Perla on a very reliable tip from one of his informants who reported that a subject called "Chilo Bomba" was responsible for the recent shootings causing the death of a child. Chilos real name was Iginio Garcia. He ran errands for the boss of La Perla who considered him loose cannon. The informant had located Chilo in a house on the corner of Lucila Silva and Triburcio Reyes Street.

David split the team in three with him and Fernando taking the lower road, Tiburcio Reyes. Hector and the rest of the team were going to cover Lucila Silva Street. Three uniformed patrol officers with Maranda cover the exit at Matadero Street.

As David and Fernando approached Chilo's house they saw one of his men pull out a shotgun. David stopped and reversed the car quickly getting out of range. They both got out of the car and took cover. Fernando pulled out an M16 rifle from the trunk of the car and took cover.

"Fernando, I know how elusive this bastard can be. Keep your eyes on the back door. He might try to give us a slip", David said.

"Chilo come on out. I have an arrest warrant", David called out.

"He is not here! Get out of here you bastards" the man with shotgun said as he fired a shot.

"Drop the damn gun and come down ***now***", David said.

"Don't shoot", and he dropped the shotgun and started walking. All of a sudden he pulled out a pistol and fired 2 shots at David missing by a couple of inches.

Fernando shot the guy and asked, "David, you OK?".

"Yes, I am OK", David said.

David and Fernando walked over to inspect the body that was lying dead on the ground. As they walked up to the house where Chilo was living they heard several shots. Then a loud thundery shot was heard.

A few minutes later Hector called and said, "We have a problem. A sniper plugged Chilo in the head. Also, we had to shoot two of Chilo's body guards."

"Hang in there I called forensics. I have one dead here also. I'll have forensics stop by you first", David said.

David and Fernando searched the house where Chilo lived. They found cocaine, heroin, marijuana and lysergic acid. One of the Forensic teams inventoried and bagged everything.

David went over and talked to Hector.

"Listen, I have to go and talk to Lacquer. I need you to do the paperwork on Chilo and his two buddies", David said.

"No problem. You want me to do the paperwork on your stiff? Hector asked.

"No Fernando wrote that one up. Thanks anyway", David said.

David and Fernando went then to the corner of Boulevard Del Valle and Tanca streets to a big two story house surrounded by an eight foot concrete fence. It had an electric gate and two cameras focusing on the gate and the street and a button and loud speaker. It was the house of the reputed boss of La Perla Antonio "Tono Bemba" Lacquer. He was six foot five inches, had dark skin and was always very well dressed.

David pressed the button and a voice came over the loud speaker "What do you want"?

"I am Lt. Gonzalez and I need to speak to Don Antonio please"

"Wait", the voice said.

Then minutes later the voice said, "The car, the guns, the radio and recording devices stay out of the gate. You alone Lieutenant are to come in".

The gate opens with enough space for David to come in. Two men thoroughly searched him. He was then escorted to the study where Mr. Lacquer was sitting behind a beautiful ornate mahogany desk with a matching credenza. A very comfortable sofa as well as two chairs were neatly place in front of the desk, but David wasn't invited to sit.

"Don Antonio, I apologize for the interruption. I know you are busy man, and I thank you for seeing me," David said.

"No apology necessary. What can I do for you?" He asked

"I have some bad news. Chilo Bomba is dead. Shot apparently by a sniper", David said.

"He who kills by the bullet dies by the bullet. Chilo was not bad but he went crazy and started shooting and hurting innocent people. Sooner or later he was going to get bumped", Don Antonio said.

"I just wanted to let you know, just in case you find out anything and wanted to share is me", David said.

Don Antonio said, "It's your watch. It's your operation. I thought you guys did it".

"He was more valuable for us alive. He had information he wanted to share with us", David said.

"That is just too bad that you lost your source. Let me make it clear that I had nothing to do with his demise. He had lots of enemies and it was bound to happen", Don Antonio said.

"Well, I don't want to take any more of your time sir", David said.

"Have a nice day Lieutenant", Don Antonio said.

Chapter 25

I was invited over to the Immigration and Naturalization office by Inspector Franco. I was surprised at the call to come and interview a detainee.

"Hi Robin, how is it going", Franco said.

"It's going, I don't know where but it's going", I said.

"Yes, I guess we all feel like that sometimes especially when Washington keeps changing the rules of the game", He said.

"Yes, we've got some guys that make policy on the run causing all kinds of hiccups". I said.

"Let me tell you what I have. The vice squad raided the bars and most of the women lawyered up. Anyway, the police had called us to check on the foreigners whose papers were not in order. We picked up a few and are sending them to their respective countries. This one has a student visa. I think she could bring some useful information. At first I did not believe that she was a student. I found out that she is second year actively registered. I felt sorry for her. She did mention some information on some of the women who work as mules. So, I leave the ball in your court", Franco said.

After looking over the paperwork we went into the conference room where the young lady was sitting. She was 24 years old brown hair medium build. I introduced myself and asked her name.

"Me llamo María Eugenia Montes" she said.

"Where are you from?" I asked.

"I come from Pereira, Colombia. I came here on a student visa. I am currently studying at the Interamerican University", she said.

"What are you majoring in?" I asked.

"Social Science, second year", she said.

"I understand you were working at the Black Angus Bar", I said.

"Well, I don't work there. I just go to meet with some clients and make some money for rent and other needs. I am very selective of my clients", she said.

After expanding the causes of social dysfunction in the world and ways to fix it I went straight to the point.

"Tell about the men hanging around the Torreon Bar and later around the outside of the Black Angus?" I asked.

"They are two low life cafiolos (pimps) from Argentina that have a couple of women they administrate. They instill fear in them and force them to produce. They take their passports and say they are protecting them. If the women don't produce they get a beating", She answered.

"What other information would you like to share?" I asked.

"There are two women that I have seen that are more independent. They are usually together. They are not frequent at the Angus. They transport currency back to Colombia. They are from Cali", she added.

"Who are these women?" I asked.

"One of them is Vera and the other is Christina", she said.

"Do you have a last name on them?" I asked.

"No we all go by just first fake name", she said.

"What is your fake name?" I asked.

"Camellia", she said.

"How do you know they are transporting currency?" I asked.

"Because I heard them talking about it twice. They mentioned they were going to the bank but I did not get the name of the bank", She said.

"I am going to need your cooperation. I am going to verify the information you gave me. I also need your help in retrieving more information. Try to find out the name of bank and when are they going to leave"? I asked.

"Asking around is a bit dangerous but I will do what I can. You got to give me time", She said.

I gave her our confidential telephone number. I established call and meet routine. With that she left the conference room.

I thanked Franco for the opportunity to meet this person and the information and I left. I got back to the office and I gave Don the information.

CHAPTER 26

An inquiry was made into the shooting of Chilo and his gang. It was determined that the shooting was self-defense. Chilo's death was considered a homicide. It was determined, by ballistics, he had been shot by a high powered rifle. The shot was fired about 200 yards away by an expert marksman.

David was called to Superintendent Calera's office in Rio Piedras. Fernando drove him there and stayed at the first floor turning in some requisitions.

David went up to the third floor and the receptionist buzzed him in.

"Good morning David, how are you?" Calera asked.

"Fine thank you sir" David answered.

"Please take a seat. Would you like some coffee?" Calera asked.

"Thank you sir I will take it black" David answered.

"Well, I read the inquiry report and I just want to know what the hell were you and your team doing in La Perla shooting around"? Calera asked.

"Well sir, I got orders from Assistant Superintendent Maldonado asking us to drop everything and investigate the shootings in La Perla. The unfortunate killing of a child caught in crossfire . . . David was interrupted by Calera.

"Stop right there! Investigating a homicide is a function of the Homicide Squad. The next time someone comes and ask you to investigate something you wait until it is cleared by me. I think we should stay focused on our main task" Calera said.

"Understood sir" David answered.

"David, something came up and I need your help. It appears that a boat came onto the shore at Salinas and got stuck on the sand in shallow water.. It seems to be loaded probably with weapons for the Macheteros. I got a call from Guayama Patrol Officer that spotted it. I told them to just observe. No interference until you guys get there". Calera said and gave David a sheet of paper with all the information.

"Will do sir I am on my way if there is nothing else"

"Go and be careful" Calera said.

David went down and found Fernando he gave him the sheet and said "We are going to Salinas to see what is on this boat".

He called the office for back up and they were on their way. Salinas is in the southern part of the Island not far from Ponce the second largest city. Two hours later they were at the spot where they could see the boat. David and Fernando stopped at a distance and saw two unmarked police cars with four persons. One of them David recognized as the Captain. They stayed at a distance where they could see a 30 foot boat that tried to come close to the reefs under cover of darkness. The load was heavy and they must have miscalculated the ability of the boat to navigate in. The boat had a name "Vida Mia" (My Life). David called Maranda and asked her to find out who was the owner of the boat. He also called Calera and informed him of what he saw and who was there.

David called, "What's your 20 Hector"

"I am over by the Barbosa Expressway", Hector answered.

"Stay there. I see a man in a row boat bringing in some packages. They are loading the packages on a white truck" David said.

"Roger that", Hector said.

"Hector, the white truck is just leaving. It might go up your way. Follow at a distance", David said.

"Roger that" Hector answered.

Maranda called back and said, "It's a 30 foot Catalina registered to a Pablo Montes and berthed at the Patillas bay. The owner works at the Patillas hospital as therapist"

David acknowledged.

Hector called David and said, "There is an unmarked police car following a white truck at a distance. I mean they are far behind. I am staying out of their sight".

"Stay far behind and let's see where this takes us to", David said.

After a while Hector called back and said, "We were pulled over by a uniformed patrol car. We lost the truck. They must have gotten off at one of the exits".

David responded, "OK, come on back. There is no sense in running around just let the team that was following take care of it".

David then went over to where the Captain was.

"What are you doing here David?", Captain Torres asked.

"Hi, we came to give you some assistance with what is going on with this boat. We are under orders from the Superintendent", David answered.

"I can care less who sent you and thanks for offering but we are taking care of this. It is under our jurisdiction", the Captain responded.

"As I said before I am just following orders and I am not here to take over. So what is going on?" David asked.

The Captain ignored the question and went to his vehicle and called the southern area commander Colonel Melilla. After he finished talking he came back to where David was and said, "We are to give you information, but the case is ours. We are making the arrest".

"OK, so what is going on?" David asked.

"We think they are transporting marijuana. I have a unit tracking a white truck which could be in route to a warehouse"

Two men in a row boat came ashore with some neatly bundled packages and the Captain and his Sargent detained them. The Sargent opened one of the packages and pulled out a brick of marijuana. David recognized it coming from Colombia.

The two men were arrested and driven to Ponce Headquarters.

Chapter 27

The Captain arrived at the Ponce Police H.Q. and had detainees booked. They refused to give their names and had no identifications. They were booked as John Do's and brought to a holding cell.

After clearing some of the paperwork the Captain brought one of the men to an interview room. With the Sergeant present the Captain said, "You have the right to remain silent; you have the right to an attorney; if you cannot pay for an attorney the state will assign you one. Do you understand?"

The detainee answered, "Yes".

"Could you state your name for the record?" the Captain asked.

The man was silent.

"Listen, things might not be too bad for you if you cooperate. We are sure you are not the owner of this cargo. So why don't you start by stating you name and address for the record", the Captain said.

The man was silent just staring at the wall.

David knocked on the door.

The Captain said, "Come in"

David came in and was standing behind the Captain and the Sergeant. The Captain asked, "Did you pick up your cargo in Mexico or Colombia?" The man said nothing.

David said, "May I ask sir?".

"Go ahead", the Captain said.

"Listen, your boat, the 30 foot Catalina picked up the cargo from another ship. All you were doing was transporting for a fee. Tell me who you were working for?" David asked.

The man said nothing.

"Your boat has already been impounded and towed away. We know where the marijuana is coming from. The quantity seized is enough to put you away for a very long time. So tell me, who are you working for?" David asked.

The detainee did not even blink so they took him back to the holding cell.

They brought the other detainee to the interview room. The Captain read him his Miranda rights.

"Please state your name for the record", the Captain asked.

"I would like a lawyer please", the detainee responded.

"I am going to need the name of your lawyer and also your name so your lawyer knows who his client is", the Captain said.

"Just get the public defender", the detainee responded.

"The Captain then said, "For the record the detainee has asked for a lawyer from the public defender's office. Sir, we have to check and see if there is one available and it might take some time. Why don't you start by giving your name".

"Just get the lawyer I will wait as long as it takes".

David was going to ask a question but decided not to. He stepped out of the interview room and went down the hall and found Fernando.

"They lost the damn truck", Fernando said.

"I know, Hector told me", David answered.

"No, I mean the guys the Captain said were following the truck. They just came in about 10 minutes ago and said they lost the truck", Fernando said.

"I should have guest", David said.

"Well, what now?" Fernando asked.

"I think we should go to Patillas and check out this guy Pablo the therapist", David said.

Chapter 28

It was mid-week and I had arrived early at the office and checked the incoming calls on the CI call in line. There was a message from Camellia. She called at 3:30 am and said "There are two leaving for Colombia tonight. They might not be together so look for one blond and one brunette. Beware they might be wearing a wig. They talked about picking up some currency before the trip"

After listening to the message a couple of times I called the airport flight control to find out the time of the flights departing to Colombia. Then I went and met with Don and Joe to give them an update on the information.

"I think you should just go to passport control and stand by the customs officer. Have him make a record so we can interview them upon return", Don said.

"I am of the opinion that we should stop them, search them, and interrogate them", I said.

"Wow", Joe said. "If they miss their flight they will get lawyered up and we won't get much out of them. Plus they will be suspicious that somebody ratted them out which will make it difficult for your CI".

"I guess you guys are right. I'll call customs to see if we can get an extra uniform agent to help out", I said.

I made some calls and got help from uniformed customs and immigration agents that were checking the outgoing flights to Colombia.

Joe and I went to the airport and spoke to the customs officer that was at the departure gate of the Colombia flight. He gave me the passenger manifest list where he circled four names of women but they did not match the description.

Just as we were about to leave immigration officer approached us. He told us that two women, one blond Maria Estela Lozada and one brunette Sara Rodriguez boarded a flight to the Cayman Island.

"So that is where they are taking the currency. I bet it's a numbered account in the Bank of Cayman Island and from there they either run back here or go direct to Bogota", I said.

"I bet the other four that went to Colombia are mules and will be here in about a couple of weeks", Joe said.

We were told to call the office by one of the immigration officers.

Joe picked up a phone and dialed the office.

"I need you guys to go to Roosevelt Roads Navy Base and check out a boat that the Coast Guard is towing in. It is a 30 foot Catalina and they were carrying quite a load of marijuana", Don said.

Joe informed Don what we found out at the airport and we went off to inspect the boat.

CHAPTER 29

Manuel Rivera called Santin and said, "I would like to meet with you to go over some errors in your tax return to see if we can come up with an agreement".

"I am in court and probably won't be out until 3:30pm. I have to go to the Caguas area, by the Pueblo Supermarket, to take deposition. Maybe we can meet up there", Santin said.

"That sounds good I will be there. See you then", Rivera said.

At 4:44 they met in the parking lot of the Pueblo Supermarket.

"What went wrong this time?" Rivera asked.

"The idiots came too close to the shore line. It was low tide so they got stuck in a sand", Santin said.

"The police have two in custody," Rivera said.

"Yes, I know. They haven't talked and they asked for the Public Defender. They probably will get out on bail if it can be arranged", Santin said.

"I understand the Coast Guard has the boat and by now they are tearing it apart. I hope they don't find anything else", Rivera said.

"Cool it. Calm down will you. We got more than half out. Col. Melilla made sure it was safe but the rest had to be impounded.

Captain Torres had no alternative because Lt. David showed up and started asking questions", Santin said

"That is not good. I think David is dangerous. He asks too many questions and he is one of Calera's favorites. Also I just found out that he has been meeting with the Federal Agents. They could cause trouble that we would not be able to get rid of", Rivera said.

"I don't think they can link us to anything. Remember we are not dealing directly with the suppliers", Santin said.

"Let's just hope it stays like that. I think we should lay low for a while", Rivera answered

"Well, I need you to go to the bank and get 300 thousand and send it to the supplier. I need an air drop of dust next week. After that we will lay low for a while", Santin said.

"O.K. then I will see you soon at the governor's ball", Rivera said.

One of David's men, Victor, followed Santin and took pictures of his meeting with Rivera.

Meanwhile David and Fernando were in Patillas at the hospital where Pablo Montes worked.

"Hi, my name is David and this is Fernando. We are from the Police" they both had their identifications out.

"What can I do for you", Pablo said.

"Are you the registered owner of a 30 foot Catalina "Vida Mia? David asked.

"Yes I am. I don't think I am breaking the law by owning a boat", Pablo said.

"When was the last time you used the boat?" David asked.

"It must have been about a month ago, why?" Pablo asked

"So what happened to your boat?" David asked

"Well nothing I hope. Why are you asking me this?" Pablo asked.

"Where is your boat now"? David asked.

"I loaned it to my cousin two weeks ago. He was going on a fishing trip up to Vieques with some friends. I think he got back four days ago", Pablo said.

"What's your cousin's name?" David asked.

"Alberto Revilla. Is he in trouble?" Pablo asked.

"What does he do for a living?" David asked

"He works at the Fuentes Fluviales power company", Pablo said.

"What does he do there?" David asked.

"He is warehouse supervisor in Cayey off of Rt. 735", Pablo said.

"When was the last time you spoke to Alberto?" David asked.

"That was about fifteen days ago probably. I don't remember the exact day. He came over to pick up the keys to the boat and some nautical charts. Could you please tell me what is going on?" Pablo asked.

"Your boat was on shallow water and got stuck on the sand over by Punta Pozuelo. They were trying to come in as close as possible to the shore so they could deliver a load of marijuana sacks. The boat has been towed by the Coast Guard to Roosevelt Roads. It has been impounded for carrying illegal substance. There are two men arrested one could be your cousin", David said.

"I can't believe this is happening. I have nothing to do with that I swear" Pablo said.

"You better do better than that. We need to know who can verify where you have been over the last ten days. I am going to need you to write down everything you can. Do it here now or you can come with me to San Juan and do it there in our office", David said.

"I will do it now while you interview some of my coworkers if that is O.K. with you", Pablo said.

"Yes, go ahead", David responded.

David asked Fernando to interview some of the coworkers while he made some telephone calls.

Chapter 30

I wanted to know if David had any information about the boat that got stuck in the sand in Punta Pozuelo. I radioed the office and asked Marta to call David. Marta radioed me back and said that David was down in Ponce. She said Police Captain Torres was handling the arrest of two suspects.

Joe and I went through the main gate of Roosevelt Roads Naval Base. We were directed to the pier where we found the sailboat tied up. After presenting our identifications we were allowed on board.

Joe stayed on deck talking to the Coast Guard diver.

"What kind of damage did it get? Are we safe or is it going to sink soon?" Joe asked.

"No need to worry. It was just the keel that got stuck on the sand because of the low tide. It was easily pulled out because it had lost whatever load it had", the diver said.

After thoroughly inspecting the cabin and the engine room I came up on deck.

"Well it looks like they cleaned everything out when they hit the dune. I could not find anything", I said.

"I was informed that they found two rifles, 30 caliber bolt action. They are registered to the owner of the boat Pablo Montes. They checked and he has no criminal record", Joe said.

"So are we going to go see Pablo Montes?" I asked.

"Let's go down to Ponce and talk to Captain Torres first. I think Mr. Montes might be there by now", Joe responded.

Joe and I arrived at the Police H.Q. in Ponce and had to wait for Captain Torres. He showed up after having us wait for over half hour.

"Good afternoon gentlemen. Sorry to keep you waiting. Please come in and sit. Can I get you some coffee or soda?" Captain asked.

"Nothing for me thanks", Joe said.

"Same here", I said

"I understand you guys did an excellent job picking up some bundles of controlled substances", Joe said.

"Yes", the Captain said with a smile. "We picked up four neatly bundled packages of marijuana in addition to what was washed up on the beach. We also have two guys in custody".

"Any information from them you would like to share?" Joe asked.

"No, I don't have anything. I know what you are thinking but they are zippered up and are waiting for a lawyer", the Captain said.

"Who is the attorney", I asked.

"Someone from the Public Defender's Office he has not arrived yet", the Captain said.

"We will wait. Can I use your telephone to call my office? Joe asked.

"Yes, you can use that one", the Captain said signaling to the telephone that was on a small table by the window.

Chapter 31

Joe, Captain Torres, the public defender and myself went to the interview room. The lawyer met first with his client then called us all in.

"For the record what is your name?" The Captain asked

"Ramiro Pacheco"

"Ramiro, you know you are under arrest for possession with intention to distribute marijuana?" The Captain asked..

"I was just transporting. I had no intention to distribute or sell. This shit is not mine", Ramiro said

"Who were you working for?" the Captain asked.

"I don't know", Ramiro answered.

"Why were you transporting the marijuana?" the Captain asked.

"I got a telephone call giving me instructions on where to go. I needed the money. I am unemployed", Ramiro answered.

"Who called you?" the Captain asked.

"I don't know. They just asked me if I wanted to work on a sail boat. I asked how much and they said it paid $2,500. They would give me half upon sailing and the other on return", Ramiro said.

"Where did you get the call?" the Captain asked.

"At home in Humacao", Ramiro said.

"Why did they call you at home?" the Captain asked.

"Because I left my telephone number with a couple of friends telling them that I needed work I am unemployed", Ramiro said.

He gave the names of his friends and where they could be found and the Captain had the Sargent take care of locating them. The Captain then, out of courtesy, asked me and Joe if we had any questions.

Joe said, "Ramiro, you know that with the amount of marijuana you brought in you will get a very stiff prison sentence. So why don't you tell us a little about who called you"

"I told you what I know. The caller did not identify himself he just said if I wanted to work and make $2,500 to go to Patillas to the pier where the boat was", Ramiro said.

"So they were going to give you the money just for showing up?" Joe asked.

"No, I was hired to do the sailing and they paid me half at the start. The other half would be paid at the end when I brought the boat back", Ramiro said.

"Where was the marijuana going to be delivered?" Joe asked.

"As I said before, my part was only to sail the boat and bring it in. I helped them unload but there was someone else, who I don't know, picking up and delivering", Ramiro answered.

"Who was that someone else?" I asked.

"I told you I don't know" Ramiro answered.

"What type of vehicle were they putting the stuff on?" Joe asked.

"I was on the boat and just came off when we finished unloading", Ramiro said.

"Who threw the other bags off the boat?" I asked.

"We were trying to lighten the load and pull the boat out of the sand", Ramiro said.

"Who was the other guy with you?" Joe asked.

"All I know is his first name Adriel". Ramiro said.

"I am sorry we have to stop my client has told all he knows", the Lawyer said.

The Captain called one of his officers and told him to take Ramiro back to his cell and bring up Adriel.

Joe took the opportunity to call Don.

"I think you guys should come back. Let the locals do their thing we have other issues over here", Don said.

"We are on our way", Joe said.

CHAPTER 32

Calixto asked Jairo and Rodolfo "How much paste do we have in our supply?"

"There is enough for production. We sent a container with 500 kilos across to the southern coast of Spain, Benidorm and Malaga. Customs agents there have been well greased so we will have no problems with that one. To the Dominican Republic we sent 200 kilos. Haiti we sent 100 kilos", Jairo said.

"What about the pinches Mexicans?" Calixto asked

"They were sent 300 kilos but they want more. We are waiting for money", Rodolfo said

"I am going to need 80 kilos packed for airdrop. Pack it tight because it might have to be sea bound", Calixto said.

"I will get it done right away", Rodolfo said. "By the way, I was told that two of the men unloading the last delivery by boat in Puerto Rico got busted by the Police".

"That, my friend, is their problem. They order, pay and we supply. So you guys go and do your business", Calixto said.

As they left Jose Antonio came into the office.

"I just got back from Santa Ana, Bolivia, and they are jacking up the price of production", Jose Antonio said.

"By how much?" Calixto asked.

"They started out at 16% and I had to talk them down to 10%", Jose said.

"Well, guess what, we are going to increase to $5,000 a kilo and a flat fee of $5,000 for transport", Calixto responded.

"The market has been shifting to a greater demand for cocaine dust and second for heroin tar. The United States has a cash cow of marijuana in California. I know for a fact that they get some also from the Sinaloa", Jose said.

"We have been exporting over 10,000 kilos a month that's why we need the damn Bolivians", Calixto said.

"Right now we are dealing in Bolivia with Eriberto Sol D'avila who owns 18,000 acres of coca leaf and several processing plants. He is also in bed with some high government officials there. He recently had several traffickers sent to Concholoro Prison. They were stealing paste", Jose Antonio said.

"Well, just be careful with that guy", Calixto said

"We have to go to Bogota to meet with Father", Jose told Calixto.

"Well, let's get going. It's a long drive" Calixto said.

"I have a flight chartered so we can leave any moment" Jose said.

They arrived at Don Manolo's penthouse and were greeted by the servant who told them Don Manolo was at a meeting and would be in soon.

An hour later Don Manolo came in and sat with them having a drink and said, "I am glad to see that business is well. So what is the latest news?"

Jose Antonio gave him a briefing on the negotiations.

"You did well in having them lower to the ten percent. You have to be careful that they don't establish a minimum purchase which might be more than we need. Also, be careful with Sol D'avila. He is sly and sometimes double deals. Make sure you stay on the good side of the Mexicans. If you slip up Sol will be moving in fast", Don Manolo said.

"Did we finish the construction of the extra classrooms for the elementary school at El Arenal?" Don Manolo asked.

"Yes and we added a state of the art audiovisual room with satellite communication", Jose answered.

They had a late dinner and they decided to wait until morning to go back to Pinos Calzos.

Chapter 33

David and Fernando cautioned Pablo Montes not to leave the Island and left with his signed statement. They drove up to Cayey, Rt.735, to the Fuentes Fluviales Power Co. warehouse.

"I am Lt. David Gonzalez and this is Sargent Fernando Velez and we are here to see Mr. Revilla please".

"He is in the office in the back. You can go right ahead", the employee said.

David went to the back and knocked. Fernando stayed out searching around pretending he was just taking tour.

"Come in! May I help you?" Revilla asked.

"I am Lt. Gonzalez, Policia", he said showing his identification.

"Please sit down Lieutenant", Revilla said.

"Did you recently use Pablo's sail boat for a fishing trip? David asked.

"Yes I did", Revilla answered.

"Where did you go?" David asked.

"I went out with a few friends on a fishing trip off the coast of Vieques", Revilla said.

"When did you leave and return?" David asked.

"We left early on Saturday and returned on Tuesday late afternoon. We berthed the boat in Patillas", Revilla said.

"Did anybody take the boat after that?" David asked.

"Not to my knowledge. I secured the boat and left the key where we always leave it in a compartment on the side. We do that so the key is available in case Pablo loans it to someone", Revilla answered.

"Do you know if anyone was to make use of it"? David asked.

"I wouldn't know. What is all this about?" Revilla asked.

"Earlier today the boat got stuck in a sand dune when it was unloading a ton of marijuana. We currently have two persons in custody and they are now probably in front of a magistrate spilling their guts trying to get some kind of a deal. So you, your cousin, and your friends are all suspects", David said.

"Now, wait a minute. I have nothing to do with that. I used the boat, then brought it back and berthed it. Why don't you ask Pablo who he loaned it to?" Revilla asked

"This is what you are going to do. You are going to write out a statement containing everything. I need the departure hours and return hours; where you went; where you anchored; what you saw; what you fished. Also put down the name, address and telephone of the men that went with you. Write anything else you might want to add for your benefit. Make sure it is all the truth because if there are inconsistencies there might be serious consequences. You have the option of writing it out now or you can come with us to our office and write it there"

"I will write it here".

David stepped out of the office and found Fernando.

"There is enough places here where you can hide quite a load, but the place is clean", Fernando said.

"Are you sure about that?" David asked

"Hey, you know me. I checked every corner", Fernando said.

"Shit! I smell fish and I think they are sharks", David said.

"I would bet there is a cover up and it is high above our pay grade", Fernando said.

"I agree. I am going out to the car to radio the Superintendent. Keep an eye on Revilla. Make sure he gets everything down or else we are taking him with us", David said.

"No problem", Fernando responded.

David went to his car and radioed Calera and explained the situation and after they reviewed the statement written by Revilla they left.

Chapter 34

"I didn't think you guys were going to get too far in Ponce", Don said.

"I think we should have gone to Patillas to shake up the owner of the boat", I said.

"That would have been another waste of time. The locals have the information and we are getting a copy. We can bring the guy in at any time for questioning", Don said.

"So what are we doing here Don?" I asked.

"Containment", Don said.

"Sorry, but I think the suits in Washington have it wrong again. They made the same mistake in Vietnam and we came out with our tail between our legs and now we are losing it again. The economy here is down the tubes. The unemployment is 18% higher than any state. That's why these people will take the risk and transport it, sell it and kill for it", Robin said.

"Look, I understand your frustration but we have to follow policy and procedure. Just hang in tight. We will soon turn the tide around", Don said.

"Robin, for some time we have observed that there is high ranking official corruption in the south. We know there is something going on at the police and probably at the prosecutor's office", Joe said.

"This might have been a good opportunity to uncover some dirt", I said.

"Some of these guys are just messengers. But the people at the top will slip and when they do, we will be there to bring them in", Don said.

"I know David was out investigating this case. I will give him a call to see if he can fax us what he has, "I said.

"I would be careful with David. He sometimes is a loose cannon look at what happened to Chilo Bomba", Joe said.

"Wait a minute, how do you know it wasn't the other way around", I said.

"I know you have been in the same situation but what we're saying is be careful", Don said.

"O.K. Listen up. Call came from Customs at the port. There is a container they think might have something in it and they asked for our help. Andrew and McIntire are there now. I want you guys to go over there and help them out", Don said.

"Are they going to open the container there?" Joe asked.

"The suggestion is a surveillance to see who picks it up and where they will take it", Don said.

"O.K. we are on our way".

We arrived at the Port of San Juan, which was full of containers, and went to Bolin's office.

"Hi Bolin! What's going on?" I asked.

"We have a container with a possible false wall. We did a visual inspection and it looked like there were some gaps on the inner wall. We tapped on the outside in the back it sounded empty. I requested a search warrant and we are waiting to see who comes to pick it up. I understand that you are going to follow to the delivery point", Bolin said.

At that point the radio in Bolin's office crackled and they heard Andrew say "Hey we are rolling and it looks like he is going on Rt. 28".

"Roger that. The following team is on its way", Bolin said.

Joe and I followed and we saw Andrew turning on to Rt. 165.

"Look, he is turning on Mendez Vigo Street. You think he is going into the town of Dorado?" I asked.

"I don't see why unless he is going toward the town of Vega Baja", Joe said.

"He is making a left turn on Rt. 854 and Andrew is slowing down", I said.

Two miles later the rig stopped at a warehouse and backed into a loading dock. The driver got out unhooked the rig from the cab. Then he got back in the cab and left. We waited for hours until we saw a tan Mercedes Benz car enter the parking lot. Genaro Causa and two men went in the warehouse.

"Let's wait until they start unloading the container", Joe said.

Chapter 35

"There is something fishy about the Ponce area", David said.

"What do you mean by that?" Calera asked.

"There were two guys bringing marijuana inland from the boat that got stuck in the sand. I think there might have been two others who vanished with most of the cargo. Captain, Sergeant and their men were waiting for the men to come ashore. The guys that had most of the cargo got lost", David said.

"I gather you are upset. But, anyway you might as well know, that the two guys that were arrested have posted bail. They are probably gone by now", Calera said.

"Two of my men that were following the truck got stopped by a pair of uniform police in a patrol car. That made them loose site of everything. By the way, who was the prosecutor at the bail hearing?" David asked.

"It was Santin. I understand he did put up a fight at the bail hearing", Calera said.

"I would like to have somebody keep an eye on him", David said.

"I don't mind as long as it is done discreetly. Keep me out of it", Calera said.

"OK. I will probably have Victor start watching Santin. He is very good at undetected surveillance", David said.

"I also think that there is someone up here in the metro area that is connected to this mess", Calera said.

"Do you have any hunches?" David asked..

"Not right off the bat. Listen, I have a report that a small aircraft made a couple of low circles around Boqueron bay two nights ago. I think it was a drug drop. There was a fast boat picking up whatever they dropped", Calera said.

"Shit, we are getting airdrops again. Has anyone reported anything from the Mayaguez office?" David asked.

"I have no reports" Calera said.

"I will see what I can find out", David said.

David left Superintendent Calera's office and drove to his office.

"Fernando and I are going to Mayaguez to see what the scoop on the air drops is. Hector I need you and Victor to go to the courthouse in Ponce and find out about the bail posted for Ramiro and Adriel. Maranda I need you to contact the Coast Guard and see what's going on with the boat", David said.

It was late afternoon when David and Fernando arrived at the Mayaguez Police station. They went to the narcotic investigations department.

The officer in charge greeted them and gave them a copy of the report.

"A person that was out for a late night stroll saw an airplane circle at a very low altitude and then takes off again. He thought the airplane was going to crash", the officer in said.

"Did he see any boats out there?" David asked.

"He did not pay too much attention to it. But he thinks there were some fishing boats out. There is always some fishing going on", the officer said.

"Has anybody reported any floating objects other than the normal?" David asked.

"No floating objects reported. I think the maritime unit is out. I heard they were almost by the Mona Passage. The Carnival cruise is due to go by there tonight", the officer said.

"We are going to be in the area for a while so keep me posted. You mind if I use your office to call the Superintendent?" David asked.

"Go right ahead", the officer said. I have to go to records. Make yourself at home"

David called the superintendent and then called Robins office and talked to Don.

CHAPTER 36

The men that got out of the Brown Mercedes Benz were in the warehouse turning on the lights. One of them was opening the bay doors.

"Hold on", Andrew said, "They just opened the loading dock door. I think they're going to start unloading the container".

"I just saw a man open the trunk of the Mercedes Benz car", Robin said.

Meanwhile, in the warehouse, Genaro told the men to take the furniture out of the twenty foot container.

"Be careful this is fine mahogany and I don't want it nicked", he said

"What's going on Andrew?" Joe asked

"It looks like furniture is being brought into the warehouse. Do you think we should hit them now?" Andrew asked.

"No. Not yet. Let's give them a chance to move some of the furniture out", Joe answered.

They were moving some credenzas, desks, dining table tops with the legs separate well wrapped, and bed headboards.

"I think they have penetrated deep enough so let's go and take down this operation", Andrew said

"Hold on", Joe said. I just saw them put something in the trunk of the car".

"Roger that", Andrew said

"Robin and I will take the inside", Joe said.

"Mac and I will take the container and the car", Andrew said.

Holding his I.D. up Andrew said, "Federal Agents we have a search warrant. Stay where you are".

Genaro was inside in his office. He picked up the telephone and called his lawyer quickly.

I went into the office and told Genaro "Federal Agents with a search warrant. You can put the telephone down".

"Excuse me I am trying to run a business here. What is this about?" Genaro asked.

"I will be searching the office. Step over here please", I said.

"I don't know what you expect to find. All I have here is furniture. I have the paperwork for it. It's been stamped by customs upon entry", Genaro said.

"You will soon find out when we find it", I said

"I want to call my lawyer", Genaro said.

"You'll soon be given the opportunity", I said.

McIntire was inspecting the trunk of the car and said "I just found a bundle of what looks like kilos of cocaine"

Joe said "I'll go out to the car and help Mac. Robin, you better secure Genaro".

"O.K" I went over to Genaro and cuffed him and said you are under arrest and gave him the Miranda rights".

I took Genaro to the container where Andrew discovered four packages that looked like cocaine. He was going to test and make sure it was cocaine.

Don had arrived and was in the container with Andrew. "I was talking to the boss in Washington and he sends his congratulations for a job well done. We've contained this before it gets out on the street", Don said.

Genaro said "That stuff is not mine. I don't know who put that in the container".

Don said, "By the way Robin, the Mayaguez police called. The cruise ship sting will most likely go down tonight. I told them we would send someone to meet them when the ship arrives at San Juan".

They loaded Genaro and the two men working for him in the van that Don brought. He drove them to the office. Pictures were taken documenting the location of the cocaine. When the search of the premises ended they loaded the cocaine in the Mercedes Benz and drove to the office where they would store it in the evidence lockup.

CHAPTER 37

The marine police unit had been following far behind the Carnival Galaxy cruise ship and scanning with infrared. This was the fourth time they were following one of the Carnival ships and nothing had happened with the previous ones. They thought this would be the one because they had spotted some boats that did not look like fishing boats.

"This is Marine Police101 the speed boats could be entering by Rincon or Anasco", the skipper of the marine unit said.

"Roger that", the shore police responded.

David informed Calera that this could be the one that dropped the drugs. Calera called the coast guard who had a cutter nearby and had flown a helicopter to the airport in Mayaguez. David and Fernando met and boarded the helicopter and waited to hear from MP101.

"I see a compartment is open on the rear of the ship. One of the speed boats is trailing close. This is it they are doing the dumping", MP101 radioed.

"Roger that", shore units responded.

"Affirmative we are on our way" the helicopter pilot responded.

The Coast Guard cutter was about a mile away near the Desecheo island area. The ocean was rough and the current tight. The cutter had sent a message to the cruise ship to stop.

The helicopter was on top of the cruise ship with its search light on the ship. David asked the lift master to lower him and Fernando down.

"The wind is strong it could be dangerous", the lift master responded.

"I don't care we need to catch them in the act so go ahead and lower me down", David said.

"O.K." he then clipped David on and sent him down first. It looked at first like David was going to land in the water. The wind kept swinging him and the helicopter had to correct its course. He was finally caught by one of the crew members of the ship before he almost fell in the swimming pool.

Fernando was next and made it down all right.

"Where is the Captain of the ship?" David asked.

"He is up at the bridge right now", the crewman said.

"Take us there please", David said.

They went up to the bridge where the Captain had just called security.

"What in the hell is going on? Who the hell are you guys? As captain of the ship I have the authority to put you under arrest", The Captain said.

"Sorry to cause the inconvenience sir. I am Lt. Gonzalez and this is Sargent Velez with the Police of Puerto Rico. We have observed that there have been several packages from you ship tossed overboard. We suspect that its content is drugs".

"That is nonsense. How dare you come up with that accusation?" the Captain asked.

"Could you take us to the stern of your ship please and call your security team to secure that entire area and not let anyone out please?" David asked

The Captain made his call and then they proceeded to the stern of the ship.

"There is one boat speeding toward Anasco. I think it might be empty. The other one looks like it is going to hit the area of Aguadilla. That one might be carrying a load. We are picking up some bags floating", MP101 radioed.

They arrived at the stern of the ship storage compartment. The ship security officers had secured the area and had detained four members of the crew.

"Fernando, we are going to need the work identification cards and passports from these four gentlemen. We are going to need to question them thoroughly", David said.

"Yes sir will do", Fernando responded.

Meanwhile David, the ship Captain and security chief were inspecting the cargo area.

"I got to get the ship the ship going again", the Captain told David.

"Go ahead sir the Coast Guard cutter will tag along", David said.

The shore was reporting that the boat speeding toward Anasco made a quick turn toward Rincon. It was beached and the crew made a run for it. The boat speeding toward Aguadilla was beached in Aguada. They managed to offload several bundles of marijuana into a truck they hijacked and headed inland

CHAPTER 38

The interrogation room was prepared and Andrew and McIntire went in with Genaro and his lawyer.

"You have the right to remain silent; anything you say can be used against you; you have the right to have an attorney present" Andrew said as he started the interrogation.

"State your full name and address for the record please?" Andrew asked.

"Genaro Causada. I live at 1250 Yagrumo Street, Guaynabo".

"Where do you work?" Andrew asked.

"I own and operate a furniture import business in Rio Piedras and rent the warehouse in Dorado", Genaro said.

"Do you get most of your furniture from Colombia?" McIntire asked.

"No, some comes from Brazil and others from Europe", Genaro said.

"Who did you purchase the cocaine from?" Andrew asked.

"That is not mine and I don't know anything about it", Genaro answered.

"We found twenty kilos loaded in your car. Was that your first delivery?" McIntire asked.

"My client has no comment", the lawyer advised.

Meanwhile Joe and I were in Don's office discussing some options.

"This is the opportunity to hit some of the traffickers with a delivery bust", I said.

"Washington says we should prosecute Genaro and his men and get rid of the dust", Don said.

"We can still get rid of the drugs and at the same time get rid of some of the riffraff that was expecting a delivery", I insisted.

"It would look very good for statistics if we could bust some of the puntos de droga (supply points)", Joe added.

"I checked with Washington and they said to stick to the containment. We have no manpower they said", Don replied.

"That's a lame excuse. I am sure we can get some trusted local support and make it happen", I said.

"Trusted local support, I doubt it" Don said.

"Look Don, we all understand we have to play ball with the suits in Washington. We don't want to get you in trouble. Let me coordinate this on my own. If it goes well you get the credit if I mess up I get the boot and you can say you didn't know anything about it" I said.

"O.K., give me an outline of your plan and I will consider it and if it is good I will take the chance", Don said

"You're on", I said.

Joe said, "Count me in".

The results of the first round of interrogation were not producing the results expected because the lawyers had silenced their clients.

CHAPTER 39

Two of McAllister tug boats met the Carnival ship to guide her into the San Juan harbor. A group of immigration officers and members of David's squad came off the tug and boarded the ship to start processing the crew members that were in custody. There were four in custody at the moment. They were the ones that work in the storage area. The storage area had a garage size door. When opened at port a forklift could deliver bulk supplies. Of the four crew members in custody two were from Colombia, one from Miami and one from Venezuela.

Fernando had collected all their passports and ship identifications. He started interrogating the crew member from Miami.

"State your full name sir?" Fernando asked.

"Gabriel Alcazar", the man answered.

"How long have you been with the ship?" Fernando asked.

"Two years", Gabriel said.

"Have you always worked in the supply storage area?" Fernando asked.

"No, I worked in maintenance for a while, then I got transferred to the storage area", Gabriel said.

"Do you like working at the storage area?" Fernando asked.

"Yes, it's hard work but I like it", Gabriel answered.

"Where did the ship stop for supplies?" Fernando asked.

"We loaded up when we left Puerto Rico and we resupplied in Cozumel, Mexico", Gabriel answered.

"Any place else you picked up supplies?" Fernando asked.

"No just Cozumel. We pick up fresh produce and fruit", Gabriel answered.

"What else did you pick up?" Fernando asked.

"That is all I know", Gabriel said.

"How many bags of marijuana did you load in Cozumel?" Fernando asked.

"I don't know what you are talking about", Gabriel answered.

"Come on, we have the bags you shoved out that door (motioning to the garage door that was closed now)", Fernando said.

"I don't know what you are talking about", Gabriel said

"You are going to be charged with conspiracy to transport controlled substance with intention of distribution for sale", Fernando said.

"I do have a right to lawyer?" Gabriel asked.

"Yes and you have the right to remain silent and if you can't afford a lawyer the court will appoint one for your defense", Fernando said.

David had finished his inspection.

Maranda and Hector were testing some cannabis residue that was found on the floor of the storage area near the door.

David had the crewmember from Venezuela escorted to the area where he wanted to interview him.

"State your name please?" David asked.

"Alejandro Cárdenas from Caracas Venezuela".

"How long have you been working on the Galaxy?" David asked.

"Six months only. I transferred over from another ship that went to dry dock", Alejandro said.

"Have you always worked in the storage department?" David asked.

"Most of the time especially when we are receiving at port", Alejandro said.

"Were you working in the storage, receiving merchandise in Cozumel?" David asked.

"Yes I was there for a while but then I was sent to take the lubricants down to the machine room", Alejandro answered.

"How many bags of marijuana did you load on to the ship?" David asked.

"Don't know anything about that", Alejandro answered.

"Listen, it would be to your benefit to cooperate could save you a lot of trouble", David said.

"I really don't know what you are talking about" Alejandro said.

"You are going to be charged with conspiracy to transport and distribute controlled substances with intention to sell it. You have a right to remain silent; you have the right to a lawyer and if you can't afford it the court will appoint one", David said.

David left and went and talked to Arnaldo, a Federal Agent from the Bureau of Narcotics.

"Are you going to charge these four men in Federal Court?" David asked.

"I just called the AAG and he said that because of the maritime activity they will arraign in Federal District Court of San Juan", Arnaldo answered.

"I'll call Superintendent Calera and tell him we are turning everything over to Federal Bureau of Narcotics", David said.

"Did your support team pick up some of the marijuana they were dumping?" Arnaldo asked.

"Yes, I will have them send pictures now and ship the evidence properly to your office", David answered.

"Thanks David, I appreciated it".

Chapter 40

Calixto asked Jairo "What the hell is going on at the coca plant?"

"They are picking coca leaves out of our fields at a rate of 750,000 to process 1000 kilos of cocaine. The demand for cocaine is growing. We are going to have to get some more paste from the Bolivians", Jairo responded.

"Shit, I was trying to keep that at a minimum", Calixto said.

"Remember we agreed to purchase enough paste for at least 1,000 kilos so we have to live up to our agreement. If we don't want start a war", Jairo said.

"I know, I know. How did the shipment to Miami go?" Calixto asked.

"We sent 200 kilos by fishing boat and transferred it to a ship that was entering the Miami River and successfully dropped off in the area of Smile Shipping", Jairo said.

"What about the money?" Calixto asked

"Some in Cayman Island and the rest telexed to Hong Kong account", Jairo answered.

"What else do you have in mind?" Calixto asked.

"We were running short of some of the supplies. I had to order some benzene, sodium carbonate, and hydrochloric acid to make our paste. The ship will arrive in Cartagena tomorrow and we have trucks on the way and they will take it directly to the plant" Jairo said.

"Good job be careful. Now scram I got work to do". Calixto said

Jose Antonio entered the office and Calixto said "we need to talk".

"What's up bro?" Calixto asked.

"There was a sting in Puerto Rico and they bagged one of our good customers. I heard they got Causada and some of his men as well as the container with the dust. I thought we had someone in customs office there that was going to rubber stamp it free to go", Jose Antonio said.

"Well it did not happen and I am afraid we lost our contact in customs office", Calixto said.

"Who was our contact here dealing with them?" Jose Antonio asked.

"Rodolfo has been visiting them and paying them off" Calixto said.

"Best if you keep Rodolfo away from Puerto Rico for a while until some of this blows off. Oh, by the way, the Mexicans got stung on their cruise venture off the coast of Western Puerto Rico", Jose Antonio said.

"Yes, I heard it was a good cargo of marijuana from those bastards in the Gulf area", Calixto said.

"So what's the plan?", Jose asked

"We are going to continue to have airdrops in Puerto Rico when the steam blows off. We increase the airdrops in the Dominican Republic. There is a secure area where they pick up the drugs. They drive them down Rt.4 to Boca Yuma where they load it on boats. It's an easy run across to the west coast of Puerto Rico. If necessary they can make a pit stop at Desecheo Island but stay away from Mona Island. We are also making some selective drops in Haiti. I am not too happy with Haiti because they want to control us and not so good a paying", Calixto said.

"Sounds good but the old man says to be careful with what you do with Puerto Rico. Also, he suggests we tie up loose ends in other words call in the shooter", Jose Antonio said.

"I know, I know. Tell him it will get done. By the way, where is our father now? Calixto asked.

"He is in Barcelona with the Minister of Finance and the Minister of the Interior in the ribbon cutting of the new stadium", Jose Antonio said.

Don Manolo had all the flower arrangements for the event brought in a special airplane. It was being rubber stamped by the Spanish customs. Jose Antonio has slipped 200 kilos of cocaine to be picked up by one of the traffickers that covered the area of Barcelona-Santander.

CHAPTER 41

The plan was presented to Don and he was not convinced it would work. Genaro Causada had agreed to cooperate but he wanted something in return. He identified Rodolfo as the point of contact from the Cali group. Rodolfo set up the meetings in different hotels of the area. They were never held in the same place.

"Genaro can contact Rodolfo and explain that I am taking over the operation. It would be giving continuity to the business", I said.

"Yes, but Rodolfo isn't going to go for it that easy", Don said.

"I think we can pull it off if we drop a few names of people that are waiting for the drugs. Genaro can convince them there is a need for a large quantity of dust", Joe said.

"That's fine, but money is the question here. I don't have the amount of cash that is needed for this. I am going to have to ask operations in Washington", Don said.

"We are going to need an initial purchase of about 150 to 200 kilos",

Joe said.

"We need to find out what the going price for a kilo is", Don said.

"According to Genaro he is getting a deal at $24,000 a kilo but they charge for delivery and also for the payoff they make", I said.

"Well you are talking about tree to four million in cash. I am going to have to do a lot of convincing to the people in Washington", Don said.

"Let's not ask for the money yet until we find out if we can make the contact. Once we have the meeting we will know what the price will be", Joe said.

They left Don's office and went to the detention center and met with Genaro, his lawyer, and the AAG (Assistant Attorney General)

"I gave you Rodolfo so what else do you want from me?" Genaro asked.

"We are going to need you to contact Rodolfo and tell him you are out on bail. Tell him that you are still in business and that you want to have your partner meet with him for a purchase", Joe said

"What is in it for me?" Genaro asked.

"Well you know we have 200 kilos of cocaine that were in your possession. You could get 30 or 40 years of prison", the AAG said.

"The stuff you confiscated was not for my use. It had owners. All I did was transport. I will accept probation without jail", Genaro said.

"Look, you are going to have to serve something. I am sure I can get you a reduced 5 years and probation after that. You would be in a federal facility away from here and in protection. When you get your probation we can arrange for you to be relocated if that is what you want", the AAG explained.

"O.K., Give my lawyer all the details and I will sign on. What do you want me to tell Rodolfo?" Genaro asked.

"Let's call now and tell him that you made bail and are keeping a low profile but that business must go on. You have a partner that is taking over. His name is Reginald and they call him Reggie. Reggie wants to meet and make a substantial purchase", Joe said.

"And can you give me a list of the people that were supposed to get the 200 kilos?" I asked.

They had a secure phone and the call was made. They were all listening in. It took a few coded words for Rolando to take the call.

"Look, I don't think it's good to do business now Genaro", Rodolfo said.

"Come on Rodolfo. Reggie is my partner. It would be like doing business with me", Genaro said.

"Puerto Rico is burning hot now, Genaro. And I am not talking about the weather", Rodolfo said.

"I am laying low and Reggie is not known to the authorities Rodolfo. It would make a good profit also", Genaro said.

"I never say no to your money my friend", Rodolfo said.

"Look, why don't I have Reggie give you a call in a few days. You will have some time to think about it. Unless you want me to contact some folks that are up in Medellin", Genaro said.

"My friend, I want you to call me in four days", Rodolfo said. And he hung up.

So they all decided to meet back in four days to make the call.

Chapter 42

I was sitting in my apartment living room looking out the picture window. I can see the night lights that illuminated the tall hotel, apartment buildings, the churches and lampposts. My apartment is close to the airport so I hear aircraft coming and going. The beach is about five minutes walking distance and I have only taken a dip in it twice. The living space is small only a one bedroom studio modestly furnished.

On the dining table I have a caneca (glass flask) of Ron Palo Viejo and a bottle of cold India beer to chase the shots down. I don't do this often but tonight I just felt like reminiscing on the endemic social problems of this island.

Years ago there was a profitable sugar cane business that produced over 900,000 tons of sugar. There were over ten sugar processing plants called centrales. I had read that the export of tobacco leaf was also on a high. There was plenty of employment even if they were low paying jobs. The local agriculture was producing enough to render a profit. The federal government was sending in supplemental food for the poor which was about half of the population. I think they called it EL MANTENGO.

Then there was a change in socio-economic structure with the establishment of industry and factories. Agricultural work was losing its popularity. Old sugar cane cutters died out and young people were running to the factories which paid more. Large sugar cane crops were broken down into suburban housing communities. Then the sugar cane and tobacco were outsourced to South America at a cheaper production cost.

Over the years the island has experienced a growth in population. It created a separation in class with poverty at a high and more people on welfare.

The industrialization brought about what I would consider a cultural genocide and a socio-economical deformity. It opened the field for drug trafficking using the island as a diving board to bring drugs to the mainland.

After the Korean War there was mass migration to New York. Some went seeking jobs and others to attend college. Over the years some of the children of these people got a little cocky and decided to play big time hoodlums running drugs and guns.

So far what I have seen here are some small time punks. They come from New York, Miami or Chicago and get themselves established at a caserios (public housing development). There they bully someone out and take over their territory. They are the capos of the housing and now they will traffic and shoot and not get caught. That is my assessment on the caserios. Probably, if I have a couple more drinks I will have the inspiration to solve the entire drug problem and I will be able to go back to New Mexico as a retired civil servant.

CHAPTER 43

Don, Andrew and the AAG had an extensive interview with Genaro in order to get affidavits for every transaction recording the date, time, location, and amount of cocaine involved in the transaction. They made a list of persons present at the transactions and all other details necessary to complete the arrest warrants against Genaro's clients.

After reviewing all the information with the AAG it was decided that there was a need for a joint operation. A meeting was held with Superintendent Calera and the Director of the Narcotic Division. Calera included David in the meeting. The plan was for all the arrest warrants to be enforced simultaneously.

Before the raids were to take place Genaro had requested a bail hearing. The AAG was not in favor. In order to set up the plan that Joe and Robin had for the buy bust they needed to have Genaro visible in his furniture store. So, a bail was set and an ankle bracelet was facilitated to monitor his movements.

Joe, the AAG, Genaro and I were at the furniture store placing a call to Rodolfo. The telephone had rung several times and there was no answer. They waited and called again and no answer. Then the telephone at Genaro's desk rang.

"Genaro how is business?" Rodolfo asked.

"Furniture always sells well", Genaro answered.

"I called you two days ago and there was no answer so I thought you were out of business", Rodolfo said.

"Sorry about that, I must have stepped out", Genaro said.

"I am glad you can tip toe out that easy. You should have Reggie answer the telephone for you", Rodolfo said.

"Reggie was out running errands and again I am sorry I missed your call. We are still in business aren't we?" Genaro asked.

"The white cabinet you want to purchase is is on back order.

Let me get back to you shortly when I have it available", Rodolfo said and hung up the telephone. I was not too convinced about the telephone call so Joe and I went back to their office. "I think the call was made just testing the waters to see if Genaro was on bail", Joe said.

"Well bottom line is that Washington is giving the entire plan second thoughts" Don said.

"The people in Colombia are not going to feel motivated for a two or three kilo sale. They move hundreds", I said.

"I understand and I will try again to convince the people in Washington. I have to go up there day after tomorrow. But as it stands it's a no go guys, we don't have the money. By the way I met with Calera and the ADA and we are going to participate in the raids. I think it is best to have one of us in each group", Don said.

Calixto was not happy with the call from Genaro to Rodolfo. He was glad Rodolfo was cautious enough not to agree to do business with the so called Reggie.

Don Manolo had arrived at Pinos Calzos and was in his study with Jose Antonio and Calixto.

"I don't think it's a good idea to do business with Genaro's associate. It's a trick from the Americans and they will do anything to get their hands on us", he said.

"I told Rodolfo to stay away from Puerto Rico. I didn't like the fact that he threatened to do business with the people in Medellin", Calixto said.

"I am not worried about the people in Medellin. In fact, I think Jose Antonio should go and talk to them and we should work together. The market is big enough", Don Manolo said.

"I was thinking about that. We are stretched too far and I am sure they can cover some of the territory that we are not actually in", Jose Antonio said.

"I agree but be careful they are aggressive sharks. Calixto, I think we should tie up loose ends in Puerto Rico", Don Manolo said.

"We have a person that can do that and is on her way", Calixto responded.

"Just tell Rodolfo to keep stalling on the calls until you have your person do what they have to do and then have them take a vacation", Don Manolo said.

"I got it covered" Calixto said.

CHAPTER 44

There was a message for me on the CI line. Camellia had called and wanted to meet at 2:00 pm. The meeting was to be held at Café Palin. It was a small coffee shop about two blocks away from the Interamerican University Campus in Hato Rey. They opened for breakfast at 7:00 am and served quick lunches between 11:00 and 3:00. After 3:00 they only served coffee, sandwiches and soft drinks. No liquor was ever served which made a nice family atmosphere.

I arrived at 1:55 pm and asked for a cup of coffee. I sat at a table in the back facing the door. At about five minutes past the hour Camellia walked in and looked around and was about to leave when I waved her in.

"I am sorry sir. I did not recognize you. The last time we met you were dressed in formal business attire", She said

"I wanted to blend in with the students and locals that's why I am wearing jeans and t-shirt. The books here on the table are for you. They are both social science related novels", I said.

"Thanks for the books sir", Camellia said.

"Inside the top book there is an envelope for you. Don't open it now. It's a little token of appreciation to help with next semester's registration", I said.

"Thank you so very much. I did not know what I was going to do for the next semester because I was short of registration money", Camellia said.

"Can I get you something to eat or drink?" I asked.

"Just coffee with milk and two sugars", Camellia said.

"So, tell me, what is on your mind?" I asked.

"The two persons that had flown out the last time I called you are back. They were in Miami and came in two days ago. There were others that came in from the same area, Miami, and I heard they are splitting up", Camellia said.

"What do you mean by splitting up?" I asked.

"Some are going to a horrid place in center of the island called Aibonito. There are no rooms to work and the act of sex is performed out in the back of the building in the open. You are supposed to lay on a cardboard box that is on a wooden platform", She said.

"Why are they going up there?" I asked

"They were told to go cool themselves so they won't attract attention. Another one left for Ponce to Isabel la Negra's bar. This one I think is a courier. I heard her mentioning distribution of kilos and collection of money", She said.

"Do you think they are going to be moving some cash again?" I asked.

"The two that came in together are getting ready to go back out. I heard them talking about dividing some cash", She said.

"What do you mean by dividing some cash?" I asked

"I am sorry. What I mean is that each one carries money", She said.

"Can you find out when this will happen?" I asked.

"I will try my best", She said.

"Do you know if they are going to use a bank?" I asked.

"I have not heard anything about a bank. I did see one of them, Vera, coming out of Banco Real in Santurce. I was on a bus so she did not see me", She said.

"Good job! I don't want you taking any risk and if you feel threatened back off and call me right away. I don't want anything to happen to you", I said

"Yes, I understand", She responded.

"Now we should not leave together. You probably should leave first" I said.

"Yes, thanks again sir", she said and left.

Chapter 45

It was early Monday morning, 1:00 am, and our meeting points were spread out in different locations. I was assigned to work with David's team by choice and we were meeting at his office in San Juan. Our target location was La Perla.

"There are two targets in la Perla. Hector, Maranda, Victor and these four policemen will go to calle San Miguel and arrest a dealer called "Pildorita". He has several bodyguards and they are armed and trigger happy. Fernando, Robin and I with these five policemen will go to calle Triburcio Ryes and arrest a dealer called "El Chavo", David instructed.

We all synchronized our watches and set out in unmarked vehicles. We were to approach our targets at the same time using the element of surprise.

The bodyguards did not expect us and they were subdued without any incident. We found Chavo lying in bed half naked and it looks like he had been drinking and snorting.

"Hey, Chavo, you are under arrest", David said as he grabbed him by an arm and pulled him out of the bed. I picked up a pistol and a shotgun from the bed and bedside table.

"No shit man, get the hell out of my face or I will blow your brains out", Chavo answered.

David held him face down and brought both arms to his back and cuffed him and read him his rights. We found cocaine, heroin and a few other firearms which were all tagged as evidence. The radio was cracking with conversation from Hector.

"David we had a problem with two of the bodyguards over here. They pulled automatic rifles and wounded one of our support policemen. We had to take the two bodyguards out and had a hard time getting to Pildorita", Hector reported.

"Roger that. Have you contacted forensics?" David asked.

"Yes, we did there is an ambulance here and forensics just arrived", Hector said.

"See you at headquarters", David said.

We drove to central police headquarters in Rio Piedras where all of the persons arrested were photographed and fingerprinted. After all the paperwork was finished we went to the magistrate on call who remanded the arrested to jail pending preliminary hearing. We went back to police headquarters to catch up with Hector. We caught the information coming that the ops at Lloren Torres, Nemesio Canales, Campo Rico and others in the area were successful. I heard there were problems at Santiago Iglesias and Cantera in Ponce. That was to be expected. Mameyal in Dorado was not as troublesome as caserios Juana Matos and Coqui in Catano.

We had been working for over twelve consecutive hours with the help of lots of caffeine. It was a little after 2:00pm and we were back at David's office on our final debrief. We were treated to lunch of a nice "sandwich cubano" brought from Panaderia El Roble. The sandwich was loaded with pork, ham, two types of cheese, lettuce, tomato, onion and a garlic mayo.

"Well what do you think Robin?" David asked

"If this works out some of the puntos will a lot of catching up to do", I said.

"I don't think it'll take long for someone to step in and take everything over. This is like fighting a cancer where you take most of it out but it comes back and kills you", David said.

"We seized enough cocaine, heroin, marijuana, money and firearms and with Genaro's testimony they will get some good jail time", I said.

I went over to Maranda and said "Hi".

She just gave me a nod and stared at me.

"Well, is it just going to be hi? Do you have something on your mind you would like to share?" she asked.

"Well, the last time you said I talked to much and you didn't like me asking questions", I said.

"So", she said.

"Well, I don't know what to say I . . ." I got interrupted by her.

"Why are you so lame? Just ask the question and get it over with", she said.

"Would you honor me in having dinner with me?" I humbly asked.

"Yes, I will. Just give me call when you are available to see if I am free", she said.

"Thank you . . . thank you very much. I will call you", I said.

After we talked for a while I went back to my office which was in walking distance of David's office.

Don called me to his office and said, "Genaro and his wife Clara were murdered at the store this morning. The surveillance team reports there was a woman visiting shortly after opening. She was about 5'7" dark long hair below her shoulders, brown pants, and a white blouse. They had just opened the store and it looks like she did not stay long. The shots were execution style two shots in back of the head probably with suppressor. We don't have much to go on as of description but we are trying to make a composite sketch" Don said

"I guess it does not get any better" I said and left Don's office.

Chapter 46

Manuel Rivera and Candido Santin met at La Fortaleza, the governor's mansion, for the governor's ball. It was a formal black tie event with a full orchestra playing soft boleros and danzas. Due to the nature of the event and crowd they could not discuss business. Santin had discreetly messaged the need to meet. Two weeks later they met at Plaza las America's shopping mall.

"Hey Candido, what is going on? You look like shit", Manuel said.

"Oh man, it has been rough lately. I had to investigate a murder in Cantera housing which was obviously drug related. Then, a jealous wife decided to stab her husband to death. Finally, last night, I had a double murder in Santiago Iglesias housing", Santin said.

"I think you need a vacation. Well, let me give you some good news. Our last three deliveries came by without glitch. The dust was of good quality and it sold without any problem. Our source says there is more demand for it", Manuel Rivera said.

"We might have a problem with air drops. They are installing better radar equipment at the base in Salinas. It's operated by the Air National Guard", Santin said.

"Can we pay them to look away?" Manuel asked.

“I have been trying to get an idea of their shift. They have 21 persons working with each shift consisting of six technicians and one supervisor. It’s too many men and someone could spill the beans”, Santin

“I understand it might be risky. The pilots are going to have to fly lower to try to avoid the radar”, Manuel said.

“I guess you heard of the murder of Genaro Causada and his wife”, Santin said.

“Only some rumors. I have not seen anything officially”, Manuel said.

“I am sure it was the Colombians in retaliation for his arrest”, Santin said

“Are you sure? I think it could have one of the customers that did not like the fact that Genaro ratted them to the police”, Manuel said.

“Yes that could be. Anyway, we have to be careful not to fall in disgrace with our suppliers. I will let you know how everything goes with the radar”, Santin said.

Victor had followed Santin at a distance and took pictures of him meeting with Rivera. After Santin left, Victor went back to San Juan and reported to David.

“David, Santin met with Manuel Rivera and after went and met with Pablo Montes. He also went to the Fuentes Fluviales warehouse twice to meet with Revilla”, Victor said.

CHAPTER 47

I left a message for Camellia to meet me at Café Palin. Meanwhile I called David but was informed that he was not available to try back later. It was afternoon so I went to the Café and sat at the same table. Camellia was late and I was about to leave when she rushed in.

"Sorry I am late but I got stuck in a project meeting at one of my classes at college", She said.

"Can I get you something to drink or eat?" I asked.

"Just coffee please, thanks", She said.

I got up and got her some coffee.

"How have you been?" I asked.

"Fine, not much going on lately", She answered.

"I have something important to ask and hopefully you can help me. We are trying to locate a woman we think is Colombian. She is about 5'7", long black hair down over her shoulders. We suspect she murdered two persons", I said.

"A white woman 5'7". There are a few that fit that description", she said.

"Do they have long black hair?" I asked

"That might not necessarily be the real color or length of her hair. Remember what I told you about wearing a wig as a disguise.

The person you are looking for could be blond or brunette and wore a wig. Also the person could be 5'2" and be wearing five inch heals", She said.

"Can you think of anyone who could be capable of doing the shooting?" I asked.

"Can you tell me where the persons that were murdered got their drugs?" She asked.

"He was getting his drugs form Cali", I answered.

"I know Vera and Christina are from Cali but there is another one that came to the Black Angus twice week before last. I think she went to Aibonito. She is called Alicia. She is about 5'6" and looks pretty muscular", she answered.

"So, she is not one of the regulars?" I asked.

"No, I have never seen her before", she said.

"If she comes back or you hear anything about her let me know", I said.

"Yes, I will call", She answered.

"Do you have any news on the ones that are going back with the money?" I asked.

"Nothing yet but I heard them talking about taking a direct flight to Colombia or going back to Miami to take the flight there. I am guessing they either have a contact there for safe travel or they need to collect some more money", She said.

"Well, let me know what you hear. Don't take any risk and remember, if you feel it's not safe give me call", I said.

"Yes I will and thanks again for the coffee", she said and got up and left.

CHAPTER 48

I walked into my office frustrated that I wasn't able to find anything out from Camellia. I tried to call David twice but the receptionist kept saying he was not available.

"Come let's go over to Customs. They are bringing in a fishing trawler with some interesting cargo", Don said.

So I decided to tag along with him and Joe. We walked across to the U.S. Customs building. It was on Puntilla Street just about a block away from our office. It was a brick building with a Spanish tile roof and had its own pier. I saw the trawler coming in and to my surprise David was standing at the front with Fernando covering the rear. Maranda was at the helm bringing it in.

"Is that Maranda at the helm bringing the trawler in?" I asked.

"Yep, that's the "wonder woman" Maranda. She learned how to navigate real well with her father who was a ship pilot. She is really good at it but did not want to follow in her father's footsteps", Joe said.

The trawler was moored perfectly and the paramedics jumped in right away and brought Victor, one of David's men, out on a stretcher. He was followed by David and Fernando. The coroner went on board and brought out two body bags. Hector and two other officers brought out six prisoners to which the U.S. Marshalls were going to take to the federal detention center. We all pitched in helping the officers unload 66 tons of marijuana. All evidence was photographed and packed neatly in a truck which was escorted by U.S. Marshalls to the incinerator at Palo Seco.

"Superintendent Calera got an anonymous tip that there was trawler named "Ivan" under a Venezuelan flag approaching the island off the coast of Culebra. He called me and we got on the police helicopter. He also called the commander of the Air National Guard and two helicopters were dispatched. The sailors in the trawler fired some shots at the helicopters but the helicopters fired back and they had no choice but to surrender. The trawler had a crew of eight Colombians. Two of them died in the firefight with the helicopters", David reported the AAG.

After David was debriefed they went to Fernando, then Hector. Maranda was last because she was making sure the trawler was secured.

"I hear you were trying to get in touch with me", David said.

"Yes, I wanted to talk to you about something. But you are busy now", I responded.

"I have to go to the hospital to see how Victor is. If you walk with me to my office we can talk", David said.

"Well, you know Genaro and his wife were murdered" I said.

"Yes, the Superintendent has the report and gave me a copy", David said.

"I believe the woman that visited Genaro just before his death was Colombian from Cali. She might go by the name of Alicia and is probably hiding in Aibonito at a . . ."

"I know where it is" David interrupted. "Do you really think she is the one that got to Genaro?"

"It's the only thing I have and I was hoping the surveillance team could identify her", I said.

"Let me see what I can do. Talk to you soon" David said and left to the hospital.

Chapter 49

David went to Superintendent Calera and gave him an additional report on the 66 tons of marijuana seized. In the report it also included information on the large fields of marijuana growing in Puebla and Guerrero, Mexico. It was noted that the traffic of opium was still steady.

"How is Victor recovering from the gun shot?" Calera asked.

"Much better since it was a clean shot in the left arm", David said.

"Give him my regards. I hope he is back soon", Calera said.

"You know we were having some surveillance on Assistant Prosecutor Santin. I have here a report on our findings. (David gave him a copy of the report) Santin met with Assistant Secretary of Treasure Rivera on two occasions, once in Caguas and the other in a parking lot at Plaza las Americas' mall. He also went up to Patillas and met with Pablo Montes. He visited and met with Revilla at the Fuentes Fluviales warehouse in Cayey. It is my opinion that he was involved in the smuggling of the marijuana that was seized on the sail boat over by Salinas", David said.

"Be careful remember he is a prosecutor and could say he met with these people because of the cases he is prosecuting. Also, I don't think you know the two guys that were arrested on that seizure; Ramiro Pacheco and Adriel are dead. They were murdered execution style one shot in the back", Calera said.

No, I didn't know that. I know that it could be that he is investigating those murders but I still have my suspicions"' David said.

"Well, I don't know", Calera said.

"Sir, just because he is a prosecutor he is not above the law. I think we should bring him in for questioning", David said.

"I think you should wait and keep on the surveillance. I think he will slip at some point", Calera said.

"What about Rivera, the guy from the treasurer office?" David asked.

"I think he will slip before Santin. Maybe you should keep an eye on him also", Calera said.

"I will get someone on it. Also, I have the description of the last person visiting Genaro at his store on the morning he was killed. It matches that of a Colombian woman called Alicia. As far as we know she might be hiding at a prostitution bar in Aibonito. We are going to pick her up for questioning", David said.

"Better hurry up you know these people fly out at the spur of the moment", Calera said.

"We are on it. Do you have anything else sir?" David asked.

"No. Good luck and be careful", Calera said.

David went back to his office and he sat down with Hector, Fernando, and Maranda and discussed the need for surveillance of Santin and Rivera. Maranda would take Rivera and Hector would take Santin. David and Fernando were going to Aibonito.

Chapter 50

David and Fernando went to the town of Aibonito. Aibonito is town located in the central mountain region of Cayey. Its temperature, being cooler that than other cities, makes it appropriate for the cultivation of coffee, tobacco and flowers. There are a couple of factories which employ most of the people that are not in the agriculture business.

The bar is called "La Cantina". It is located in the suburb called Algarrobo. It is a part cinder block and part wood building. The inside there are five tables and a Wurlitzer jut box. The counter is "L" shape with a display of bottles lined up against the wall. The owner, Pepe, is half Mexican and half Spanish, so they say. He was short light brown skin black eyes and a full head of deep black hair. His wife, Antonia, is from Honduras she is a legal resident with a green card. The wife deals with the women that come and go and there is usually about four. Farmers and workers come frequently to drink and survey the new arrivals.

"Hello Pepe, I am Lt. Gonzalez and this is Sergeant Velez" he showed his ID.

"All my paperwork is in order and I will get it for you . . .", Pepe said and was interrupted.

"No, no I am not here to close you down yet. I just need to ask you some questions", David said.

"Well, ask away", Pepe said

Fernando was at this time behind the counter checking the bottles and the area.

"Have you had any women arriving recently? David asked.

"Not really we rarely get women wanting to come to this part of the country to work", Pepe said.

"Come 'on Pepe, I don't have time for this shit. I know how crowded you get with the farmers and workers on weekends", David said.

Pepe looked back and saw Fernando pulling bottles from the stand behind the counter and said "All right, there are four women and they stay at the small cabin that is right up the hill. They should be here any minute now".

"When did they arrive?" David asked.

"They have been here for a while but two of them arrived a week ago", Pepe said.

Where are they from?" David asked.

"I don't know, South America I guess. You have to ask Antonia she deals with them", Pepe said.

Antonia came out of the little kitchen in the back and said "What do these pendejos want".

"Hello Antonia take a seat please" David said

"I don't want to take a seat I don't know anything", She said.

"Hey boss, there are a few bottles of pitorro (moonshine) and by the smell I would say it's about 100% alcohol. Should we pull his license and close him down?" Fernando asked.

"It's up to Antonia if she does not sit we might have to close it down and arrest them", David said.

Antonia was about 5', slender, short blond hair with native features of her homeland. There was sweat on her brow and she was wearing an old apron with a dish towel hanging out of the pocket. She sat down and said "What the hell do you want"

"The ladies you have up there in the cabin where are they from?" David asked.

"They should be on their way down here because I have to feed them. They are from Argentina, Venezuela and Santo Domingo. If you are looking for free sex come back later and I will hook you up with which ever you want", Antonia answered.

"We are not here for that", David said

"That's what your cops from Ponce want all the time", Antonia said.

The women arrived and were a little bit shy and about ready to leave when Fernando blocked the door and David asked them to sit.

"What is your name?" David asked the one from Santo Domingo.

"Domitila, the call me Lila", she said. She was short and of darker skin than the others.

"What about you?" David asked the one from Venezuela.

"Petra", she said smiling. She was medium height medium built with black hair.

"I am Gloria", the Argentinean said. She was blond small and thin.

The other one was shy and nervous and he asked her "What is your name". She looked at Antonia and the rest then said "Esperanza Almeida". She was the youngest probably in her early twenties short red colored hair and very white skin. David then asked, "where is the Colombian that came up here about a week or so ago. She is medium height black hair and goes by the name of Alicia".

They all looked at each other and then at Antonia.

"Her marido (that is what they call pimp) came for her she paid and left", Antonia said.

"Did anybody see the marido?" David asked

Nobody said anything then Pepe said, "He had rough features and I could tell he was armed because I saw the bulge under his shirt".

"What was he driving?" David asked.

"A red Toyota corolla. I was watching making sure he did not take anything that wasn't hers", Pepe said.

"Thank you very much all of you. Go on about your business", David said as he and Fernando left.

When David got back to San Juan he called me and said, "I went to Aibonito and I hate to tell you the woman had already left about three days ago"

"I guess she is out of the country by now", I said.

"Either that or she is hiding someplace around here", David said.

"Well, thank you", I said and hung up.

CHAPTER 51

Don Manolo had a penthouse in Malaga, Spain, off of Paseo Pablo Picasso which was one of the main streets near the beach. The apartment covered the entire area of the top of the building and you needed a key for the elevator. It had a front terrace overlooking the beach and a rear breakfast terrace overlooking Malaga. Inside it had six bedrooms and four full bathrooms. The dining room and living room were furnished in modern style and the décor was contemporary. His study was equipped with modern television and stereo imported from Hong Kong.

Don Manolo had invited the Spanish Finance Minister, Lopez de Haro, who had insisted he needed to discuss something important. "I am glad you came down and I hope you are enjoying the relaxation. Can I offer you a drink?" Don Manolo asked.

"Yes, I will have a scotch on the rocks, thank you. And, yes, I have had a good time and it has been very relaxing", Lopez de Haro said.

"What is it that you wanted to talk to me about?" Don Manolo asked.

"Well, with the death of General Franco the King is now the head of state you know. We are converting into a democracy which means we will have a parliamentary constitutional monarchy", Lopez said.

"Yes, I knew something like that would happen. I guess you will have dozens of political parties campaigning", Don Manolo said.

"Well yes, that is going to be something we are going to have to deal with. But, what I really wanted to tell you was that we have increased our partnership with the Americans and there are some new extradition rules in place", Lopez said

"I heard about that and I am glad Spain is moving in a more progressive direction", Don Manolo said.

When the minister left Malaga Don Manolo chartered a flight to Casablanca Morocco where he had a small villa. He called Jose Antonio.

"I just had a conversation with Lopez de Haro and he said Spain is making amendments to the extradition laws because of their ties to the United States. I think we must consider this as a warning and take it seriously"

Jose said "How does this affect our shipments?"

"They must continue but we must be extremely cautious. Anyway, Morocco has no extradition treaty so if things get hot we can use it as a base of operations." Don Manolo said.

"I will advise Calixto and we will be very careful" Jose said.

Chapter 52

I was in the office reading the daily blotter about Pacho Quenepo who was shot fourteen times in the Cantera housing project Ponce. Pacho was a kingpin mover and shaker in the area. Someone got greedy and decided to get him out of the way. The next story was the arrest of Zenon in Campo Rico housing in Santurce with one kilo of cocaine and his pistol, a PPK. The pistol had been used in a murder of one called Nilo in the same drug point. I went over and checked the CI phone and I had a message from Camellia.

She called at 4:04 AM and said" It looks like you will get lucky tonight at the airport. Two women will leave in the 6:45 pm Iberia airlines flight to Colombia. They will be carrying money".

I replayed the message then erased it. I went to Joe and asked him to come to the airport with me. We went in Don's office to let him know our plan of action at the airport.

We arrived at the airport two hours earlier and went to see who was checking departures from INS. Franco was there on duty today. I explained what we were looking for and he contacted a female customs agent for assistance.

About half an hour before departure, two ladies came to the Iberia airline counter. They were very well dressed and manicured with two pieces of expensive luggage. Their Colombian passports were turned over to immigration and Franco asked them to follow him to a conference room behind the counter. Joe and I had pulled their suitcases out of the conveyor and brought them to the conference room.

"Please sit down ladies we will be brief" Franco said.

"Why are we here? Our papers are in order sir" the blond said.

"May I have your name please" Franco said

"You have my passport. It's Sara Rodriguez" the blond said.

"So you must be Maria Estela Lozada", Franco said to the one with black hair.

"We are doing a random check of luggage so we are going to search your luggage in your presence. May I have your keys please?" Joe asked.

"No sir. Do I need to call a lawyer? I don't see a warrant for the search?" Sara asked.

"I am terribly sorry for the inconvenience. We will try to get you out of here so you don't miss your flight", Joe said.

"I want to see the warrant" Sara said

"We don't need a warrant. Here is the regulation that authorizes the search. So, please hand over the keys or I will have someone force the locks open" I said.

"Here are the keys. We have nothing to hide", Sara said.

The first suitcase was check and the female customs inspector said it was clear. The second one was opened and after going over the underwear, shoes, and cosmetics the inspector pronounced it to be clear also.

"Wait! Pull everything out of the suitcase. I want it totally empty", I said.

Once it was empty I started knocking on the bottom. I pulled out my pocket knife and cut the lining and pulled the false bottom out and, bingo, I found neat stacks of $100 bills. I did the same thing to the other suitcase and found more stacks of $100 bills. In total there were 400 thousand dollars.

"Did you fill out a declaration of currency?" I asked.

"We did not know the money was there", Sara said.

"I don't believe you. You ladies are in real trouble and have some explaining to do", Joe said.

"I did not know that money was in my suitcase", Estella said crying.

"Shut up Estela! No, we did not fill out any papers because we did not know the money was there", Sara said.

"Where did you get the money?" I asked.

"I said we did not know the money was in the suitcases", Sara said.

"Well, as I see it you each might get twenty years of prison", I said.

"Listen, we were given the suitcases and told to pack our belongings in them", Sara said.

"Who gave you the suitcases?" Joe asked.

"A man dropped them off at our place. I don't know his name", Sara said.

"What did he look like?" I asked.

"He was tall, with dark hair and a scar on his left check", Estela said.

"What were your instructions when you arrived to Colombia" Joe asked? "After passing customs, we were to meet our transportation and they would take it from there", Sara said.

"We are going to miss our flight. Please let us go", Estela said. "We need to take the suitcases with us. If we don't, we are dead and so is our family", Sara said.

"You are going to have to call your contact and tell them you missed your flight", I said

"That is not acceptable. They will send someone after us here", Sara said.

"This is what I want you to do. Put an in emergency call to your contact in Bogota. Tell them that it was not safe to make the flight. You are going to make other arrangements. Tell them the suitcases are safe", Joe said"

That won't work. They will not believe us", Estela said.

"Who is the person that is going to receive his money in Colombia?" I asked

"A ruthless man they call Cuchilla who works for El Atisbador. I am sure they both have people working for them here, but I don't know them", Sara said.

"What is the money from?" I asked.

"I don't know that. You would have to ask who ever put it in the suitcases", Sara said.

"Well, I want you to make the telephone call to your contact now", Joe said.

Sara was brought to a non-traceable landline to make the call. Joe was listening in as the telephone rang several times and finally someone answered.

"Oigo, quien es?" the voice asked..

"It's Sara, who am I speaking to?"

"Who do you want to speak to?" the voice asked.

"Cuchilla if he is there", Sara said.

"This is he. Where are you?" Cuchilla said.

"We are in Puerto Rico. We can't make the flight it's not safe" Sara said.

"Puta madre que te pario. Who do you think I am, a pendejo? You better get your sorry ass on that airplane or you know what will happen", Cuchilla said

"The airport is crawling with police and we risk being caught", Sara said.

The line went silent for a minute the he said "Listen bitch, stay in your apartment. Someone is going to come by and pick up the suitcases. You better have them or you know what will happen", Cuchilla said.

"Who is coming to pick them up?" Sara asked

"None of your damn business bitch just have the suitcases ready", Cuchilla said.

"Ok" she said but the line had already gone dead.

"We are going to go to your apartment and wait for the person that is going to pick up the suitcases ", I said

Chapter 53

"Chingada madre que la pario carajo. These women are conspiring something and I am going to find out", Rodolfo said

"Get it solved one way or another. We can't afford to let them fall in the hands of narc agents", Calixto said.

"I will make some calls on the secure line and get it solved", Rodolfo said.

Rodolfo called Severiano, also known as Chumita, who was the contact in Puerto Rico and said, "There is a problem with the women and the suitcases. I need you to go to their apartment and retrieve them".

"Yes, I will go right now", Severiano said.

"Wait Chumita, don't rush in. It might be a trap. Have one of your men check the place out. Then call and have them bring the suitcase to you at a safe place" Rodolfo said.

"We will get it done", Severiano said.

Severiano called a policeman called Javeco that was on his payroll.

"Javeco I need you to go to 1106 Ashford Avenue, Apartment 3A and knock on their door to see who answers. It should be a woman", Severiano said.

He gave the description of the two women.

"I want you to say that you are investigating a domestic disturbance that was reported. Then go knock on the door of other apartments and say the same. I want you to be on the lookout for narco agents. Do you understand?" Severiano asked.

"Yes, I do I am on my way", Javeco said.

Javeco had a vehicle similar to the police unmarked cars and he drove to the location and parked a block away. He went up to the apartment and knocked. Estella opened the door and stared at the police.

"Yes, what is it?" Estella said.

"Good evening miss. I am sorry to disturb you but we had a call about a domestic disturbance. Is everything all right?" Javeco asked.

"It was not us everything is fine", Estella responded and closed the door quickly.

Javeco checked the other apartments to dispel any suspicion then went to out to the street and pretended to write. He observed the area. He got in his car and left. He stopped several blocks down at a pay phone.

"Chumita, one of the ladies opened the door and she closed it in a hurry. I think she was nervous. I did not see anyone around that looked suspicious", Javeco said.

"Thanks Javeco. You did well", Chumita said.

Meanwhile Joe called and asked "What's going on? I saw a local police go in the building".

"They are checking on a domestic", I said.

"He must have had the wrong address, because he kept looking at the different buildings", Joe said

Sara received a call.

"Listen, I want you and your friend to bring the suitcases to Plaza las Americas at Macys on the second floor. Go to the suitcase department and request a refund", Chumita said.

"Look I am tired, just come on up and pick up the damn things yourself", Sara said.

"Sorry mijita, you know what the consequences are if you don't come", Chumita said

“Ok, pendejo. I will be there”, Sara said.

Joe arrived at the store first and went up to the suitcase department. He spoke to the store manager and explained the situation. He gave the manager five hundred dollars cash to be used to pay for the refund. The ladies arrived by taxi and I was following behind. They went up to the suitcase department and delivered the suitcases. The manager examined them and gave them a cash refund. The suitcases were lying behind the register and had not been touched. A store clerk came over to pick up the returned items and put the suitcases on a dolly to take them to the warehouse. Joe followed him and identified himself and, He asked “What are you doing with those suitcases?”

“Sir I am taking them to storage to be sent back to our warehouse”, the clerk said.

Joe called the manager and verified that the clerk was legit. He then proceeded to take the suitcases as evidence and gave the store clerk a receipt.

The store clerk went out and called Chumita and told him the agents had taken the suitcases.

Chumita called Rodolfo and said “Sorry boss, but the suitcases were empty and the American agents have the girls”.

“Cabronas thanks you, Chumita” Rodolfo said.

Chapter 54

Estella and Sara had been photographed and fingerprinted and held in lockup until they met with their lawyer and then the Assistant District Attorney. Through sobs and tears Estella and Sara explained that their families in Colombia would be killed because they were captured and talked. They only agreed to the meeting if their families were safe. The ADA had made arrangements with the American Embassy to get their families to a safe house. The meeting was held at a small room at the lockup facility where Joe and I were present also.

"You were both transporting large sums of money without reporting it for a drug boss in Colombia. We can consider that a conspiracy to launder money. If you cooperate and answer some questions I could ask the court for leniency", the ADA said.

"My clients are interested in cooperating", the lawyer said.

"Have you carried suitcases with money before? The ADA asked.

"Yes", Sara said looking at Estella who also said "Yes".

"Where did you deliver them?" the ADA asked.

"To Colombia and Cayman Island" Estella said.

"How many times did you transport currency?" the ADA asked.

"Several times to each place" Estella said.

"Who were they for?" the ADA asked.

"I don't know but the man that made the arrangements was called Cuchilla", Estella said.

Sara added, "I think he was also called Rodolfo".

"Could you explain the delivery process in detail?" I asked.

"After arriving at Cayman we were escorted to a hotel. We went to the room and took our belongings out. They took the suitcase to the bank", Estella said.

"In Bogota we were met at the airport and escorted to a vehicle where we were given a plastic bag to put our belongings in. They took the, Sara said.

"How much money did you normally carry?" Joe asked.

"We never knew because we were given the bags without knowledge of its contents", Sara said.

"Why were you chosen for this job?" the ADA asked.

"Because we could travel without problems", Estella said.

"Did you get to see Rodolfo or talk to him?" the ADA asked.

"No, we always dealt with some of his men", Estella said.

"Did you go to Miami for pickup?" the ADA asked.

"Yes we sometimes took a direct flight from Colombia to Florida. We stayed there for several month until it was time to pick up again and fly back to Colombia", Sara said.

"How was the pickup arranged in Florida?" Joe asked.

"They would bring us the bags and we were to pack our belongings. In Miami they made sure we got on the airplane without any problem, Sara said.

"Did they have any contact at the airport in Miami that would facilitate your entry or exit?", I asked.

"If they did we did not know but, yes, it was easier to move around in Miami", Estella said.

"Other than Miami and Puerto Rico, did you go to any other location to pick up?" the ADA asked.

"No, just those two locations", Sara said.

They finished the interview and the ladies were brought back to their cells.

Chapter 55

I went back to the office early that afternoon and I got a call from Camellia on the CI line. She wanted to meet this afternoon so I went to the Café Palin and ordered coffee. She soon came in and I ordered her a coffee.

"Is everything OK? Your message gave me the impression you were a little shaken up?" I asked.

"Oh, yes something happened last night", she said.

"What happened?" I asked.

"Two men came to the Black Angus last night and started harassing some of the women. They got violent with a Colombian woman. They thought she had ratted on the two women that were arrested. They were so violent that Tony Turizzi, the owner, and two of his men had to throw them out. When they were outside they got tangled up with a chulo (pimp) called Ricardo. They fought, and the Colombians killed Ricardo with a knife", Camellia said.

"Did you see the two men?" I asked.

"Yes, I saw them when they were inside the bar", Camellia answered.

"Did they see you or approach you?" I asked.

"They probably saw me, but they never approached me and I tried to stay away", she responded.

"Do you think that they know someone working at the Black Angus ratted on the two women?" I asked.

"I don't know. But why would they come to the bar looking for a Colombian?" she asked.

"I think they were just poking around trying to see if someone would point out a person. You say Tony kicked them out?" I asked.

"Oh, yes. He asked them to leave and they started arguing. His two bouncers came over and Tony put his hand on the gun he was wearing", She said.

"What about the guy that was outside? What happened there?" I asked.

"The guy's lady, an Argentinean, told him these guys were harassing the women so he made a stand. The Colombians argued and Ricardo, the Argentinian, punched one of them and knocked him to the ground. He then turned around to face the other but it was too late. He was stabbed several times", she said.

"Maybe it would be good if you stay away for a few days", I said.

"I was thinking of doing that. I have to go and study for a test", she said

"Ok, let's keep in touch" I said.

'Yes, I will and thanks for the coffee". She said and left.

Chapter 56

I called and asked for David. I wanted asked if he had any information on the murder that had occurred at the Black Angus the night before. I was told David and his team was bringing in a ship with illegal substances. I went down to Customs and found David he had just finished debriefing the AAG. Maranda was finishing with the details of securing the ship and the rest of the team with some help had unloaded 113 tons of marijuana that they seized from a 187 foot yacht "Heidi". I invited David to lunch at the Panaderia El Roble so we could have some sandwiches cubano. We met there at about 2:30 pm.

"Thanks for coming over" I said, "How is everything going?"

"I don't know. There are elections coming up in November. You know we have elections every four years to select the governor and members of the senate and the chamber. Well, there are three parties, the Popular Democratic, the New Progressive and the Independence", David said.

"No shit. What's your point? Are you on your soap box trying to lecture me on politics again?" I asked.

"No, I am setting the stage for what I am going to say", David said.

"Come on, spit it out. What are you getting at?" I asked

"Just want you to know that things are going to change after the election", David said.

"And how is that?" I asked.

"New people will be appointed in top positions if the New Progressive Party wins the elections. I am sure Superintendent Calera will no longer be there. I will probably be transferred to Vieques and our organization disbanded", David said.

"Shit, I thought your office was solvent enough to stand the electoral shakeups", I said.

"Our office was created and organized by order of the Superintendent and the new guy could issue an order and send us al carajo", (hell) David said.

"No wonder the island is all messed up when it comes to fighting crime", I said.

"So, are we going to eat or just talk?" David asked.

After we ate David said "This is report on the man murdered at the Black Angus:

Name: Ricardo "Ricardito" Arietta
Nationality: Argentinian
Passport #: AA47234156
Height: 5'4"
Weight: 161
Eyes: Brown
Status : Single

"The passport had entries to Puerto Rico, Florida, New York, Chicago, Madrid, and Stockholm, Argentina and Colombia. He received a puncture wound with a sharp object to his liver and his heart. According to what I heard, the guys that killed him were some Colombian sicarios (killers) trying to find out who turned in two women with over a half a million in cash. Ricardo was a pimp by profession and had a couple of women but they have disappeared. He was a user of cocaine and still had some of the drugs in his system", David said

"Any friends or known associates", I asked.

"He has been said to pay frequent visits to a bar El Torreon, in the company of two other guys and also has been seen in the company of the manager of the Banco Real", David said.

"Well I guess that is it. Thank you for the report the information is useful", I said.

"I have to ask for a favor. We have reason to believe that a prosecutor, in Ponce, called Candido Santin and an Assistant Secretary of the Treasury Manuel Rivera are heavy drug dealers. This is a report on their frequent meetings (*David gave Robin the surveillance report)*. I do think that Revilla, the supervisor of the Fuentes Fluviales power warehouse in Cayey, is storing the drugs when they come in. Most of the drugs are coming in by airdrops. I think Revilla coordinates them. Also, he must be in partnership with Santin and Rivera.

"I give you this in confidence and I think that once you analyze the material it might be something to present to the AAG", David said.

"Did your guys see any movement of drugs at the warehouse?" I asked.

"I went there personally with Fernando. While I talked to Revilla Fernando snooped around and he couldn't find anything. We came to the conclusion that they had moved the stuff but we had no idea where", David said.

"Why do you think they are dealing drugs other than a coincidental meeting?" I asked.

"It could have been a coincidence, but every time there was drug drop, Santin would go and meet with Revilla", David said.

"Could he have been fishing for some information on the delivery to build a case?" I asked.

"No, I don't think so. He screwed up a couple of cases and the perpetrators were released for lack of evidence", David said.

"Well, thank you for all the information. I will work on it", I said.

"Well, thank you for lunch and for having the opportunity to talk to you again", David said.

I went back to the office and called Maranda and asked her if we could have dinner tonight.

"Yes, where can I meet you?" she asked.

"Can I come by and pick you up?" I asked.

"I might be caught up here for a while. Why don't we meet at Don Pablo's in the Condado? Do you know where that is?" She asked.

"Yes, I know where it is. What time is good for you?" I asked.

"I would say around 7:30 pm" she said.

"Fine, see you then", I said.

I got to Don Pablo's and sat at a table for two in quiet corner and ordered a gin and tonic. It was 7:45 and she had not arrived. I was thinking she had stood me up. I ordered another drink. The waiter passed by my table several times waiting for me to order. I was beginning to get anxious when she slowly walked in. She was wearing a flowered sleeveless dress, four inch heels and let her hair down. I immediately got up and helped her to her chair.

"Sorry", she said. "I almost could not make it"

"You are fine. What would you like to drink?" I asked.

"Rum and coke please", she said.

We made some small talk as we ate and I did not want to fall in the trap of asking questions and provoking a retreat. Finally she asked the question I did not want to hear.

"Are you married?" she asked.

"No I'm not" I responded.

"Do you have a significant other waiting back in the states?" she asked.

I was hesitant because I felt this was going in the wrong direction. "Rob . . . you ok?" she asked.

"It's just that . . . I was interrupted.

"Look, I am sorry if it struck the wrong chord", she said

"No, it's ok" I said.

"Sometimes it's good to talk about it and get it out of your system", she said.

"I met her when we were in officer advanced training. She was a nurse. We went out a couple of times but it was nothing serious.

When I went to Nam she was there in one of the hospitals and we started dating again. She was funny, witty with steady nerves and very caring. We spent as much time as we could together. We were going to get married when we got back", I said almost chocking.

"What happened?" she asked

I hesitated again with a knot almost not being able to get the words out and said, "She died. She was killed in a Viet Cong attack.

"I am so sorry Rob", Maranda said as he put her hand over mine. "I am really sorry I should not have . . ."

I interrupted and said "It's ok. I'm ok"

We gazed at each other's drink. She was still holding my hand tight. Then she broke loose and said, "Well, I have to get going."

So I paid the bill and walked her to her car. We stood and gazed at each other under the moonlight. I was holding her hand. I came close and put my arm around her giving her a kiss on her sweet lips. I caressed the softness of her skin as she came back and gave me a kiss. We hugged and she then said, "It's ok Rob. I got to go. Give me a call".

I held on her hand then said "I will and thank you for having dinner with me"

"See ya", she said. And she drove off in her red Mustang.

CHAPTER 57

Next morning I met with Don and Joe and shared the information that David had given me about Ricardo, the guy that was stabbed at the Black Angus. I had checked with INS on any recent entry of Colombian male and we came up with negative.

"The "sicarios" (assassins) probably came from Miami or New York", Joe said.

"Obviously these guys had their suspicion that someone from inside the bar gave information lending to the arrest of Sara and Estella. I bet they are long gone and someone else will be asking around. You better tell your CI that they should stay low", Don said.

I went over the other information David gave me about DA Santin and Asst. Secretary of the Treasury, Manuel Rivera.

"The information is a start but we have no evidence that can connect these guys to drops or dealings", Don said.

"It seems like it's workable. Maybe we can try a buy-bust", Joe said.

"Let's put a plan together", Don said.

"I need to build a profile that I was Genaro's client and now I am out on a limb", I said.

We started working on the location where I was going to reside and we picked a two story house on Safiro Street in the town of Cidra. The house had a big shed in the back and it had the cover of woods on the left and the back. We rented it for six months. I needed a car and we managed to rent a Cadillac. A background with the necessary police record in Miami was established. Now I needed to establish a contact and for that we went over the recent arrest in the area. I found one that was connected the area of Cidra and had worked with Genaro. He had gotten his drugs several times from Revilla. A narrative was submitted to our central office in Washington for the approval of the Director of Operations and Deputy Attorney General. We also made a request for funding. Washington then requested that we establish an emergency plan and who was going to be the contact agent.

We asked for six million dollars originally and they were hesitant to approve our request. Washington finally approved the plan with their modifications and named it "Operation Sorpresa". They sent the money in one of their staff jets with the necessary recording equipment. Accompanying the money and equipment were the muscle I requested, Leonell Segarra and Jimmy Darius. They were both heavy set and locked like linebackers with long hair and scruffy beards. They were both proficient in all firearms and had brought with them the necessary firepower.

Chapter 58

My contact with Revilla was Octavio Johnson, alias "El Tigre" (The Tiger). He was a long time drug dealer who was in Federal Detention serving a ten year sentence. Octavio had worked moving some drugs first for Revilla and then for Genaro. He wanted a deal for his cooperation in setting me up with Revilla. The Assistant Attorney General (AAG) was considering it and worked a cooperation package which included his conditional release.

When Octavio was released he was instructed to visit Revilla and renew his acquaintance. We knew he was going to be searched so we did not load him with recording device. The meetings went well because all he did was talk about old times and test the waters. At the second meeting he let Revilla know about me being able to push hundreds of kilos to the mainland but Revilla was not interested. It took a third meeting for Revilla to agree to meet me. The meeting was held in a restaurant in the city of Caguas not far from Cidra. We talked about moving some dust out of the Island to the mainland. I explained that I purchased my mine from Genaro but after his death I was unable to get what I needed. My investors were in NYC and Chicago and I needed to get some high quality dust for them soon. He finally said he was not interested at the present and that he would let me know if we could do business.

I reminded him that I would need at least 200 kilos minimum. He said he would consider it and that we would meet again.

Two weeks later we had our meeting in a restaurant in Salinas.

"I might be able to provide 50 kilos at a reasonable price of $30,000 a kilo", Revilla said.

"I require 200 kilos minimum and I will pay the usual $20,000 a kilo", I said.

"Things have changed and prices go up", He said.

"I guess I will have to take my business elsewhere. Sorry to have wasted your time. I will take the fifty kilos but not at $30,000, I said.

"I can go down to $28,000", He said.

"No, no deal you need to do better than that", I said

"I can't go any lower than $25,000 and that is final and I need to see the money", He said.

"I'll take it. Just let me know when and where"

A few days later a surveillance team did see Revilla meeting with Santin twice. Octavio called for the next meeting and said Revilla wanted to see the money before releasing the drugs. We packed one million and a quarter in neat stacks in a suitcase and went to the parking lot of the Hilton hotel in Ponce. Jimmy was the advance team and was in the lobby of the hotel where he could see what was going on. Leonell and I were riding in the back and Octavio was driving. Half hour after we arrive two vehicles came with Revilla and his men. I got out of the car with Leonell walked over toward Revilla. He had gotten out of his car and met me half way.

"Where's the money?" He asked.

"The money is here. Where is the dust?" I asked.

"It is also here. Can we see the money?" He asked.

Leonell brought the suitcase with the money and opened it for him to see. He touched the bills and looked deep in the suitcase and finally pulled a room key out of his pocket.

"You can find the 50 kilos in a suitcase in the closet of this room", He said.

Leonell went up to the room with the test kit and Jimmy went with him to help. Meanwhile Revilla and his crew were counting the money, Half hour later Leonell came out with the suitcase and said it was high grade and the weight matched. Revilla finished counting and left. Our first purchase was done.

I had to debrief with Joe, my contact agent. We went over recordings and pictures and the plan.

"Don't take any chances. These people can be ruthless if they fear betrayal", Joe said and vanished.

Chapter 59

Santin went up to San Juan and met with Manuel Rivera at Don Pablo's restaurant where they were having lunch.

"Revilla has a new client he sold 50 kilos. He says the guy exports it to NYC and Chicago", Santin said.

"Was this guy checked out?" Rivera asked

"Yes, he's legit. I read his prior arrest records. It seems he is well connected", Santin said.

"How much does he want?" Rivera asked.

"He is asking for a minimum of 200 kilos but wants to know if we can stretch it to 500", Santin said.

"That is at least six to twelve million. You think he can swing that much cash?" Rivera asked.

"He had no trouble paying for the fifty right on the spot", Santin said.

"I need a guarantee that he will have the money we don't want to be stuck with 500 kilos and not be able to move it right away", Rivera said.

"I will ask Revilla to have him show the money or at least what guarantee of the money he can provide" Santin said

"That sounds good. Just let him know we need to see that he is solid on the cash so we can deliver", Rivera said.

"If we pull this one off we can lay low for a while and maybe I will retire someplace in Europe", Santin said.

"With the election coming up I might just retire and go live someplace else", Rivera said.

They said their goodbyes and Santin called Revilla and asked to meet him two hours later at the Ponce Shopping mall.

"Tell your new client we can get 200 and probably 500 kilos but we need guarantee of the money or else no deal", Santin told Revilla..

"I will call him as soon as I get back to my office" Revilla said

"Also, please remind him that the price is still the same that we can't lower the price because of quantity," Santin said and left.

Meanwhile, back at our office, we were reviewing the recordings with the AAG and Joe. We also looked at some of the surveillance photography of one of the meetings and the first transaction. Don came in and brought some photos taken of the meetings of Revilla with Santin and also of Santin with Manuel Rivera. Due to the success of the first transaction Washington agreed to another seven million for us to show. We called Revilla and asked for meeting at the Marriott Hotel in Ponce. Revilla and his men came and Leonell escorted him and one of his men to the room where we had the money.

"In these two suitcases there are twelve and a half million dollars", I said.

"Can I touch the money?" Revilla asked.

"Sure, you can touch it and smell it if you want", I said.

"Thank you. As soon as I have the material I will call you for delivery. You might need something larger than that car you have", Revilla said.

"I will be ready. I have done it before, remember", I said

"We will meet again", Revilla said and left..

Revilla went back to his office and called Severiano who was the contact with the Cali group.

"Severiano, its Revilla. I need some "tia nora". (cocaine)

"How much do you need?" Severiano asked.

"Can you ask them to ship southbound 500 kilos and also can I pay you $10,000 a kilo since it is a large quantity", Revilla said

"Never, you know the price is $12,500", Severiano said.

"Let's settle on $11,000", Revilla said.

"No, the lowest I can go is $12,000 and that is cutting my profits. I will do it for you as a special favor", Severiano said.

"We have a deal", Revilla said.

"I am going to need three million now and three before delivery", Severiano said

"You will have the money tomorrow", Revilla said and hung up.

Revilla called Santin "We need sevenmillion now for the five hundred kilos I ordered for you."

"I will get it. Just give me a couple of days", Santin said and hung up.

Santin called Manuel Rivera and asked him to go to the Banco Real and get seven million transferred in. After the money was transferred in he delivered the cash to Santin. It was then delivered to Revilla..

CHAPTER 60

"I got a call from Chumita. He wants 500 kilos of tia nora to be dropped in the southern part of Puerto Rico in the area of Lajas", Rodolfo said.

"Is this from his new client and is the money on the way? Calixto asked.

"Chumita had three million deposit sent to us via charter airplane it should be here soon", Rodolfo answered.

"Do you have enough packaged without hurting orders already placed?" Calixto asked.

"All orders have been dispatched and we have over a ton available", Rodolfo said.

"Are we going to use the normal delivery route for this one?" Calixto asked.

"I was thinking of loading it up on a ship and have it cross the Canal and go to Basse Terre. From there we could fly it in", Rodolfo said.

"To many variable can cause a loss of the cargo before it gets to its destination. Do you have a flight plan for getting in the Island?" Calixto asked.

"Chumita gave us the coordinates to fly into Lajas. He wants us to land on Rt. 303 where they would be waiting and we could make a quick exit", Rodolfo said.

"Well, I was thinking on using one of our tractor trailers and moving the load to Santa Marta and having one of our airplanes fly it in", Calixto said.

"Why don't we use the airplane we have parked on the landing strip in Pasto where the load is? We can fly to Maicao, where we refuel and, then fly direct to Lajas?" Rodolfo asked..

"I think that is a better choice rather than paying the Medellin crew taxes for rite of passage with the truck", Calixto said.

"I will get started on it", Rodolfo said.

The airplane transported the 500 kilos to Maicao where they landed and were being refueled when Calixto called.

"Rodolfo lets change the delivery from air to sea", Calixto said.

"Why is that?" Rodolfo asked.

"I have a gut feeling that this might go wrong", Calixto said.

"We don't have the material packaged for an ocean drop", Rodolfo said.

"We have a ship going out of Riohacha and I know we have some canisters. You can pack 25 kilos per canister. Its 957 nautical miles so it will only take two days", Calixto said.

"They have patrol boats in that area and you have to avoid the Mona Passage", Rodolfo said.

"Yes I know, but if we bring our boat close to Bahia Sucia (dirty bay) they can come out on two boats and pick everything up", Calixto said.

"I know the area. Its best if they they come down Short Road to the boat ramp. They can tie the boats to the trailers in the water when they are going to pull the cargo out tied to the boats. The trucks can pull them out of the water", Rodolfo said.

"What if they insist in testing the material?" Calixto asked.

"That could be a problem and even though the area is desolate something could screw up the entire operation. I still think we would do better with air transport. It's quick in and out. Also there is less overhead. All you would need would be the pilot and copilot who could act as loadmaster", Rodolfo said.

"I see what you are saying but the boat is going that way anyway. There is practically no overhead and if anything goes wrong it can quickly release the cargo and it will not be detected", Calixto said.

"I guess you convinced me. I have five canisters packed. We will get the rest ready and on the boat", Rodolfo said.

CHAPTER 61

The next day Rodolfo called Chumita "Tell your clients that we have a change of plan for the delivery".

"What are you going to do parachute in now?" Chumita sarcastically asked.

"Don't be funny pendejo we are sailing it in. There is a ship going that way", Rodolfo said.

"So where is the pick-up point?" Chumita asked.

"Look at your map for Bahia Sucia down south. You are going to need two boats preferably twenty five foot Boston Whalers with twin 150 horsepower motors to be able to bring the load in fast", Rodolfo said.

"How is everything packed? Chumita asked.

"There are twenty canisters each weighing twenty-five kilos", Rodolfo said.

"When will it arrive? Chumita asked.

"It sailed today and is expected there in two days. Get your radio set to the marine frequency 05A 156 3500. Their code name is "Anguila". You got that pendejo?" Rodolfo asked.

"Si, maricon. I will notify them of the change", Chumita said.

Previous wiretaps had been set in place when Revilla originally called to place the order. A tap had also been granted on Chumita's telephone and now they had traced the call to two different locations in Colombia.

"Amigo, I have great news. The delivery will be tomorrow night at Playa Sucia. You know where that is right?" Revilla asked.

"Yes, I know where it is why the change?" I asked.

"You will need two boats to go out to the ship and pick up the drugs. Unless you want it dropped and you get some divers to retrieve it", Revilla said.

"Listen that was not the deal. You said it was going to be an airplane landing somewhere in Lajas. Now you say I need two boats to do the pick-up and drag the stuff up the ramp. I never had this problem with Genaro. I think this shit is getting complicated and maybe we should call the entire thing off. I have the cash I can go to another supplier", I said.

"Well amigo, no need to get all worked up. Just think about it and talk to your investors and let me know before tomorrow", Revilla said.

"I can give you the answer right now. We are not doing business unless there are some changes", I said.

"I can't change the delivery method because the ship is on its way as we speak. So what changes are you talking about?" Revilla asked.

"For starters you get the boats and the crew to pick up the dust and drop $2,000 per kilo on the sale price", I said.

"Are you crazy mano? I can get the boat and pick up the dust but the price is set. I can't tamper with that", Revilla said.

"Well, get the boats and talk to your boss about the price reduction. In the meantime I will inform my investors about the new delivery method", I said

"Don't count on a price reduction. I will try it anyway for you" Revilla said.

Joe wanted to meet with me so he left a coded message. We met to discuss the delivery and how many men we were going to need now.

Chapter 62

Revilla had sent his team in to sweep the delivery area and hold positions. After it was all clear he came in with the boats ready for pick-up when he received a message from the ship.

"Anguila aquí tormenta costanera a seis millas avanzando". The message in code said a Coast Guard cutter was following the ship six miles behind and gaining rapidly.

"Anguila, abort delivery to continue to north port for normal carrier delivery", Revilla said.

"Roger that we copy" they answered.

Revilla moved his men and the boats out of the area so quickly surprising Joe and his team. Joe was there doing advanced surveillance figured that something had gone wrong. He picked up his walkie-talkie and called me.

"Robin something went wrong. Revilla and his men stormed out of this area and got lost. Try giving him a call to see what's happening".

"I will let you know meanwhile just stand by in case he comes back", I said.

Revilla called the contact number at my house and left a message with Leonell who I had left behind for that purpose. Leonell called the office and they relayed the message to me. I called Joe and told him what happened. We packed everything up and came back to the house in Cidra where I called Revilla.

"What the hell happened, why did you abort the pick-up? I asked.

"Sorry amigo. There was a Coast Guard cutter six miles out behind the ship and gaining rapidly. We had to abort to protect your shipment", Revilla said.

"How do you know it was the Coast Guard? What if it was a freighter?" I asked.

"The radar description was clear. The ship picked up their transmission with a police unit on land"; He said.

"What kind of police unit? I asked.

"Must have been American because the transmission was all in English" Revilla said.

"Where is the cargo going to end up?" I asked.

"Probably someplace up north. Don't worry I will let you know", Revilla said.

"Now I am going to insist in a reduction of the price for all the trouble caused . . ." I was interrupted by Revilla.

"No need to continue. I agree and I will talk to my people and I will let you know", and he hung up the phone.

I drove to the office to talk to Don and asked "Who the hell ordered the Coast Guard to follow the ship?"

"I didn't know about it until you call Joe and told him", Don said.

"So who did alert the CG?" I asked.

"I called the CG Atlantic Region Command and they referred me to our headquarters in Washington", Don said

"Who was the son of the bitch that ordered that? Who was the dumb bastard?" I asked.

"Calm down Robin. I know you're upset but take it easy. I called our office in Washington and finally found out it was the Director of Intelligence and the Director of Operations. Their rationale was that they wanted to confiscate the ship to make the agency look good operationally", Don said

"That is pure clusterfuck playing politics just like the idiots that got us all messed up in Nam. This stunt could have gotten us all killed", I said.

"Look, it was not my idea and there was nothing I could do about it", Don said

"I am sorry I screamed at you Don. I just hope they don't back out of the deal. They didn't tell me where the ship was heading", I said.

"Don't worry the CG has been recalled out of the area. The coast is clear for them", Don said.

"Let me get back to Cidra" I said and left.

I was pissed and frustrated thinking the deal was not going to go off as planned. I thought of Maranda so I gave a call to her office thinking I would just leave a message. Hector answered the phone.

"I just wanted to leave a message for Maranda", I said.

"Hold the line I will call her. Hey Randy you have call on line two", Hector called out.

"Hello this is Maranda".

"Hi, it's me Rob".

"Been hiding from me", she said.

"Nah!, just busy. Who is Randy? I asked.

"It's my nickname. So how have you been? She asked.

"Tired, overworked, you know the drill", I said.

"I don't mean that. I mean emotionally", she said.

"My heart flutters with happiness when I think about you. How to do you feel emotionally? I asked.

"My emotions are on even keel. Yes I do think of you and we should get together. I am about to hit the street so I got to go. Wherever you are be careful", she said.

"Thank you honey and you please do the same. See ya", I said.

CHAPTER 63

Chumita called Rodolfo and said, "Hey, we were not able to deliver because the Coast Guard was trailing the ship and moving in fast".

"Were they caught?" Rodolfo asked.

"No the captain radioed us and aborted continuing up the Mona Passage and got lost", Chumita answered.

"When and where will the ship surface for delivery?" Rodolfo asked.

"Revilla is working on the alternate delivery site. I will let you know as soon as I have it", Chumita said.

Rodolfo told Calixto and Jairo about the aborted delivery.

"Shit that was close. Are we going to eventually lose that cargo?" Calixto asked.

"I don't think so it's still on the ship", Rodolfo said

"Let me know if you need me to package another one", Jairo said

"As of now it won't be necessary but I know we have to send a ton to Guinea Bissau", Rodolfo said.

"We have that almost packaged", Jairo said.

"How are you guys doing at the processing plant?" Calixto asked

"We got some more paste and are refining fast", Jairo said

"Did we get the second payment on the delivery from Revilla's client in P.R.?" Calixto asked.

"We got three million and they still owe us three more", Rodolfo said.

"We need to get that money in before the delivery", Calixto said.

"Chumita told me the money is on its way should be here any moment.", Rodolfo said.

Jose Antonio was in the office when his father called and asked how everything was. He filled him in on the latest

"I am going to be in Morocco for a while and then back to Madrid. Don Manolo said.

"I am going to take the yacht on a small cruise stopping at Ponce and continuing to the Dominican Republic. I will be in the company of Gonzalo, Fabio and Carlos from Medellin. I will discuss some mutual cooperation. Carlos has some good ideas about air routes and contract pilots plus they own several airplanes", Jose Antonio said.

The yacht was an 80 foot Hattera named "Dona Josefina" after Don Manolo's deceased wife. It was registered in Panama to keep it out clear from the other business. It had eight rooms for guests and quarters for the captain and crew members. There was an office, a full kitchen, dining and reception area, and a sun deck. It was equipped with twin caterpillar motors capable of speed up to 25 knots.

"Be careful with the patrols in that area and keep it clean. You know what I mean", Don Manolo said.

"Yes sir, I understand", Jose said.

"Also keep me informed of the outcome of your talks with these people from Medellin", Don Manolo said and hung up.

Chapter 64

The yacht was sailing steady at fifteen knots while they did some fishing. They caught some red snapper and tuna which they gave to the cook for meal preparation. Drinking was a must from Aguardiente Crystal to good single malt scotch and German beer. They were stopped by the Coast Guard and were thoroughly searched but nothing found. The Captain, upon entering the territorial waters of Ponce, contacted the harbormaster. He asked for berthing permit which was granted and a location assigned. A Customs and INS inspector checked passports and the yacht. After the inspection was clear and all in order they were allowed to disembark. They went to the center of town, over by the ornate Catholic Church and the antique fire station. They took pictures and hired a horse and buggy to take them on a ride around town. They were brought back in front of the hotel Melia and went into the cocktail lounge. Jose took the opportunity to call Don Manolo.

"We are in Ponce and we will probably go up toward the Bahamas", Jose said.

"And how are our guests from Medellin?" Don Manolo asked.

"They are enjoying it very much. Fabio seems to be the quiet one he deals with a lot of the finance. Gonzalo has sort of a violent streak and Carlos is just full of ideas", Jose said.

"What kind of ideas?" Don Manolo asked.

"They are purchasing some airplanes to add to their fleet. Carlos is getting some property in the Bahamas to use as refueling for the air drops going into Miami", Jose said.

"Where are they getting their product?" Don Manolo asked

"They don't have a processing facility and they are using Bolivia. They move over a ton a week and Mexico alone requires about six tons", Jose said.

"Maybe we can do the processing and preparation and let them do the delivery", Don Manolo said.

"Yes, but there are some routes we wouldn't want to give away", Jose said

"That would require an increase in processing. We might need another processing plant. We would also need more paste", Don Manolo said.

"That would be something to consider if we could come to some sort of an agreement", Jose said.

"There are ways to convince them. We just need the right bait to catch the fish", Don Manolo said

"I see what you mean father. Let me go back and see what these guys are up to", Jose said and hung up.

After drinking eating and sightseeing for a couple of days they left Ponce and sailed up toward the Bahamas. As they were on the Mona Passage they saw the ship with the cargo on the other side of Desecheo Island.

Chapter 65

Santin and Rivera met in the parking lot of the Pueblo supermarket in Caguas. The meeting was held in Rivera's car. A listening device had been successfully installed under the dash and a surveillance team was 100 feet away recording the conversation.

"We must contact Revilla and have him go to a location different from the delivery site to collect the money", Rivera said

"Why do you think he should be at a different location?" Santin asked.

"Because 500 kilos is a lot of stuff and we should keep the money operation out of the hassle of unloading, counting and testing the material. The money needs to be counted carefully", Rivera said.

"I agree about the money being counted responsibly but I think the dust is their responsibility", Santin said

"But what if we have the opportunity to take the money and the drugs? That would give us a larger profit margin", Rivera asked.

"Don't you think that would be a little too greedy? It could backfire on us" Santin asked.

"Not if it is well planned. Just leave that part to me", Rivera said.

"I will talk to Revilla about using a different location and let you plan the rest", Santin said.

Santin went to his car and left. Rivera went into the supermarket and made a call on the pay phone.

"It's Rivera we need to talk. Meet me in the cocktail lounge of Hotel La Concha in about one hour".

"Yes sir, I am on my way" the voice responded

Meanwhile, while on his way to Ponce, Santin stopped by Revilla.

"You say the delivery most likely is coming in by Rincon. I need you to have them deliver the money at the Mayaguez Hilton. I reserved a room for you so you can do the counting of money without interruption", Santin said.

"What about the dust?" Revilla asked.

"Have them pick it up in Rincon. It will give them the opportunity to check the drugs undisturbed and give you the opportunity to do the same with the money", Santin said.

"I will have to split up my crew. Remember I have to leave two men with the boats that are going out to retrieve the dust", Revilla said.

"You can do it with four using the two that drive the vehicles and take the boats in the ocean to collect the dust. Leave the other two men, well armed, to guard. Let your customers worry about the dust. They probably want to weigh, count and test", Santin said.

"O K, I still need to contact the ship and find out when they expect to be approaching so I can get the boats ready to go. I am not going to tell our clients until the last minute", Revilla said.

"Sounds good to me. You square it out" Santin said and left.

CHAPTER 66

Manuel Rivera's special contact was Sergeant Hidalgo Mercado who was a member of the police strike force. It was a special operations group that leisurely worked and had a separate office in Rio Piedras. They were all trained in riot subversion prevention. He was six foot tall, brown skin, brown eyes, dark long hair and scrunchy beard. He parked his red Toyota Corolla on the side street and walked to the hotel. As he entered the lounge his eyes scanned from one side to the other and then moved slowly to Rivera's table.

"I ordered you a beer", Rivera said.

"What's on your mind?" Hidalgo asked.

"I have a plan where we can take possession of several hundred kilos of cocaine. Would you be interested?" Rivera asked.

"Yes, I am certainly interested. What's the plan?" Hidalgo asked.

"There is a ship bringing in a cargo of 500 kilos and they are going to drop it off at Rincon Bay. Two boats are going to go out and pick up twenty containers containing twenty-five kilos each. The guys that are receiving the drugs must test and count them before they leave. Most likely they will be driving down PR 115 to get to highway 2 on their way to Cidra", Rivera said.

"Who is this consignment coming to?" Hidalgo asked.

"It's a client of Revilla who used to get his stuff from Genaro Causada", Rivera said.

"Did you guys check this person out?" Hidalgo asked.

"Santin checked his record and said the guy is OK", Rivera said.

"So you think we should intercept before they get to highway 2?" Hidalgo asked.

"Yes, give them a chance to verify and load their vehicle. Once they advance several miles you and your men intercept. You guys are police so there might not be resistance. Just tie them up and take the cocaine and leave them there", Rivera said.

"You make it sound too easy. What about witnesses?" Hidalgo asked.

"You could always charge them using a few kilos as evidence. Or you could dispose of them saying they resisted arrest. You will think of something", Rivera said.

"What's my take on this?" Hidalgo asked.

"You can get half and I will tell you where to deliver the other half. If you have to charge them and need material take ten kilos out of my take", Rivera.

"OK, it's a deal. I'll do it. Call me with the final details" Hidalgo said.

Hidalgo left and Rivera stayed for a while. Surveillance team members that were observing them left after Rivera. They went to Joe's office to give him a report.

Chapter 67

Joe met with me and asked "How are you doing?"

"You did not come here to ask me how I am doing so tell me what is on your mind", I answered.

"Surveillance and taps have uncovered important information. It seems the ship is going to drop off the drugs in the Rincon bay. They want the money delivered to the Hilton in Mayaguez", Joe said.

"We have a tracker that we are inserting in the suitcase so we can follow the money", I said.

"You know, Washington does not want the money to be out of our site", Joe said.

"Look, the only way we can have a strong case against these people is to follow the money", I said

"Don is trying to work something out with the folks in Washington. Has the money been counted and serial numbers logged" Joe asked?

"Yes, all that is done. We are going to need help. We now have two sites to take care of", I said.

"Don is asking the US Marshalls and the FBI to supply the necessary help", Joe said.

"The people we need should look more street wise not like desk jockeys. They should be briefed on what is expected of them", I said.

"Don is taking care of that. Don't worry. They will be well prepared for the task", Joe said.

"What else is on your mind" I asked?

"My fear is that they are planning to take the material from you guys and it might get rough", Joe said.

"This is what I want done. Let them take the money and we follow them to see who comes to pick it up and arrest them. My team will leave with the drugs and expect a hit at some point. We let them take it. A mile later your team intercepts them and takes possession of the drugs. We arrest them all for conspiracy to transport and sell controlled substance", I said.

"That sounds great but what if we lose them?, Joe asked.

"My team has to inspect the drugs and test it. While doing that we insert a tracking device. It will alert you when they get on their way. A mile after they leave us tied up your team hits them and arrest them", I said

"There is going to be some shooting. They are going to try to hold onto the drugs at all cost", Joe said.

"We just have to be ready for that contingency", I said

"OK, let me get back and meet with Don and see what's up. I'll keep you posted ", Joe said and left.

Chapter 68

I got a call from Revilla late in the afternoon. I assumed he was going to come up with more excuses for delay but he surprised me.

"Amigo hope you still have my money and we can do business", Revilla said.

"I will do business if you tell me where and when but your time is running short", I said.

"No need to get hotheaded. Bring the money to the Mayaguez Hilton room 204. I will be waiting for you. The dust will be delivered tonight at the beach in Rincon off Rt.115. If you are coming up Rt. 2 get off at Rt. 115 and follow it to the boat ramp", Revilla said.

"That is a problem. I can't be at two places at once", I said

"Send somebody to deliver the money while you go pick up the dust which is important to you", Revilla said

"The money can be counted but will not be released until we verify the integrity of the drugs", I said.

"I have no problem with that", Revilla said.

"What time do you expect the dust to be ready for pick-up?" I asked,

"The ship should be in shortly before midnight. Its going to come in as close as possible to make a fast drop", He said.

"OK, my men will be there", I said and hung up.

I called Joe and relayed the information.

"I bet the ship is right now behind Mona Island and will come in fast for a quick drop", Joe said.

"I am going to send Jimmy and Leonell with a couple of guys to deliver the money", I said.

"Don't you think you should go with the money", Joe asked.

"Revilla is not expecting me with the money. That will give him a good opportunity to make mistakes", I said

"I will be with the surprise party that will be waiting for the ones that are going to snatch the drugs from you", Joe said.

"Let's play it safe", I said.

The last briefing was quick since we had seasoned agents from Customs, Marshalls and FBI. The teams were already divided and everyone left. Don, Leonell, Jim and two Customs agents were taking the money to the Hilton. Don arrived at the Hilton and went up to room 204 and knocked on the door.

"Come in amigo. Bring me some green happiness", Revilla said.

"Yes it is all here. You can count it if you want", Leonell said.

"I have two machines that will help me with that. You will see how fast it will go. I will be able to tell if you are short", Revilla said.

Meanwhile I went to Rincon and met the men that were sent with the two Boston Whalers. Two of them were already in the water with the boats. The ship had radioed and it came in as close. It was already unloading. The transfer was done without a hitch. They used the pickup truck winch to pull the trailers with the boats out of the water. We started unloading from the boats and testing before we put the canisters away on our truck. I slid a tracking device in one of the canisters and set it at the very end of the truck. When we finished we let the guys that brought the boats leave in their pickup trucks. Just as we were going to leave two vans pulled in and blocked our way. The men jumped out and said "police don't move" several times. They had their shields out so we could see them. This was it I thought. The hit came earlier than I expected. There was a tall heavy set policeman giving the orders to everyone. He looked familiar but I could not figure out where I had seen him. They left us tied up but I noticed that they split the load.

Hidalgo had secured his load in his van. He gave instructions to the other guys to take the other van to the storage facility where Rivera would be waiting in Mayaguez. Hidalgo then left in a different direction.

The men going to deliver to Rivera left and were soon intercepted. Joe and his group stopped them. After several shots fired and finally the firefight stopped. Two of the men going to deliver to Rivera were wounded. Medical attention was requested while quick first aid was applied. They were interrogated about the location of the delivery of the drugs.

Joe sent one of his men over and released me and my team. I went over to where Joe was and after inspecting the truck I realized that half of the load was missing.

"Joe I recognized one of the men that came and took us by surprise. I am almost sure he was the guy I saw driving the red Toyota that met with Maior when Mingo did the buy. I think he took half of the load in other direction. He is probably going up Rt. 2 toward San Juan", I said.

"Did you get a description of his vehicle?" Joe asked.

"No, I was tied up and it was out of sight. Call it in anyway. It's a van going up Rt. 2 with several individuals disguised as police", I said

"Are you sure it was the same person you saw with Maior?" Joe asked.

"Well, I am not absolutely sure. But, he looked like him", I said.

Joe radioed the information but by time it was transmitted to the highway patrol's Hidalgo had already reached the airport in Aguadilla. He left with two of his men on a chartered airplane to the Dominican Republic where he had a buyer for his portion of the drugs.

Joe left with a van full of men arrested taking them to the detention center in Mayaguez. I left with a group of agents and the truck to the storage facility where Manuel Rivera was waiting.

"It's about time you guys get your asses here. Where is Hidalgo? Rivera asked.

"He is not far behind making sure we were not followed", I said.

"And who may you be?" He asked.

"I work for Sargent Hidalgo and we are on his squad", I said.

"Well don't just stand there. Start unloading the stuff and be careful", Rivera said.

"How do you want it stacked?" I asked.

"Right over against this wall, neatly. Open one package up and let me see it", He said.

I pulled out one kilo and gave it to him and he opened it and tested it.

"Wow, this is good stuff", he said.

After unloading four containers I called it quits.

"Manuel Rivera we are Federal Agents and I am arresting you for possession of controlled substance with intention to sell and for conspiracy to launder money". I read him his Miranda rights.

"This stuff is not mine. I am just doing a favor by opening a storage bin. The owner of the storage facility said he would give me some cocaine for my personal use. I do not sell anything", Rivera said.

"You can explain that to the judge", I said.

"I want to call my Lawyer", Rivera said.

"You will have a chance to do that as soon as we get to the detention center", I said

When we got to the detention center the US Marshalls had two busses to transport all the detainees to San Juan for an appearance before a Federal District Court Magistrate. The press was already looking for the story to be published.

CHAPTER 69

Don, Leonell, Jimmy and the customs agents were waiting in the parking lot of the Hilton. They saw Revilla's men come out with the suitcases and get into their car. Don decided to arrest them and blocked their exit.

"Don't move federal agents! Leave your hands where I can see them *NOW* or I'll shoot." Don said

"OK, OK, don't shoot." One of Revilla's men said

"Come out of the car slowly," Don said.

"Where is Revilla?" Don asked

"I don't know who the hell you are talking about" one of Revilla's men answered.

"Listen you punk, I have no time to waste. You are all going to be charged with conspiracy to launder money from the sale of narcotics. We are also going to add firearms violation and any other thing I can find. You will probably spend the rest of your rotten life in prison. So, where the hell is Revilla?" Don asked.

"What's in it for me? one of Revilla's men asked.

"If you cooperate I can put in a good word for you", Don said.

"He stayed in the room and told us to take the money. He will follow behind us", one of Revilla's men said.

"Where were you supposed to take the money?"

"We have to go to the airport here in Mayaguez to the charter flight terminal and meet someone there. Revilla was supposed to follow behind us."

"Who were you going to see at the airport?"

"I am cooperating. I need to have a little more guarantee that you are going to put a good word for me. My name is USmail Sastre. Easy to remember like the mail you know".

"Yes Mr. Mail you are cooperating but you did not tell me who you were seeing at the airport", Don said.

"We have never seen the person. Revilla was going to identify him. But if something happens, we were to go directly to the terminal and use the code word "Areito" when we meet the man who will be wearing a blue or black suit." Mr. Mail said.

Don had sent Jimmy and a customs agent to the room to pick up Revilla but the room was empty. Don thought he was probably on his way to meet the people at the airport so he left with Leonell and a customs agent. He left Jimmy with Revilla's men. Jimmy took them to Mayaguez court where they had prearranged to use the holding cells.

Meanwhile, Revilla and one of his associates had walked out the back of the hotel. They walked to a car they had parked a block away. They drove off to Ponce to Mercedita Airport where they boarded a charter flight Costa Rica.

Don arrived at the Mayaguez airport and they went to the charter terminal and were directed to the tarmac where the airplane was waiting. Santin was inside the airplane and had a man standing at the steps.

Leonell said in perfect Spanish, "I need to speak to your boss."

"Who the hell are you?" the guy asked.

"We work for Revilla", Leonell said.

"Wait here I will go get him," the man said.

When he came back he brought Santin dressed in a navy blue suit who asked "Who are you guys"?

Leonell said, "Areito".

"Where the hell is Revilla?" Santin asked.

"He is on his way following behind," Leonell responded.

"Bring those suitcases into the airplane," Santin said.

"Do you want to check the content?" Leonell asked.

"You bet I do. Open them up," Santin said.

Once the suitcases were opened Santin touched the money. He looked in the suitcase where Revilla had taken out money. He said, "That son of a bitch took some of my money. I will get him for this. You guys better tell Revilla to pay you from what he stole from me. And now if you get the hell off my airplane I have a long trip ahead.

"We are Federal agents. I am placing you under arrest for violation of the controlled substance act and money laundering. Anything you say can be used against you in a court of law . . ." Don was interrupted.

"Spare me the speech. I don't think you know who I am . . ." Santin was interrupted.

"We know damn well who you are. Revilla has already spilled the beans on you," Don said.

"That son of a bitch. Wait until I get my hands on him," Santin said.

Santin and his associates were cuffed. The pilots were interrogated and the flight plan was registered for Cayman Island. The pilots and plane were hired by Santin. They did not know what the cargo was. They only knew that they were to fly him to the island. The pilots were detained but not charged. The airplane was moved to a separate location to be thoroughly searched. Santin, his associates and the pilots were transported to the detention center in Mayaguez. There they were processed and bussed to San Juan to appear before a Federal Magistrate.

Chapter 70

In San Juan the dance had started early at the Federal District Court. Lawyers were waltzing in as bail hearings and trial dates were being set. The Assistant Attorney General's working with us was making sure that the evidence, money, cocaine, wiretaps and testimony was in order. I was in and out of court testifying. I made several visits to the Attorney General's office handling our cases. It seemed that both, Rivera and Santin were going to be granted bail. Their lawyers were challenging the evidence and the court was being lenient which was pissing me off.

Joe came over to my desk and said "I checked the flight controllers in six airports. I found a flight plan to Costa Rica from Mercedita Airport in Ponce. It was filed and the aircraft left at 2:45 am. The other one was a flight to the Dominican Republic filed in Aguadilla".

"I guess Revilla is in Costa Rica probably on his way to Mexico and Sergeant Hidalgo is selling our stuff in the Dominican Republic", I said.

"We contacted the embassies in both places and they were working with the local police to arrest and send them back", Joe said.

"I bet we won't get any reliable information back", I said.

Don came in and said, "Col. Harrington says the Director is not too happy with the way this all worked out and he has summoned me to Washington to explain".

"Explain what?" I asked.

"I guess it's why we let two million dollars and 250 kilos of cocaine slip out of our hands", Don said.

"They are a bunch of politicians who don't know how things can go in the field", Joe said.

"I guess I should go with you so I can take some of the heat away from you Don", I said.

"Thanks Robin but it's me they want. I think there are other things they want to discuss. You guys hang in tight and hold the fort whatever comes comes", Don said.

"What do you mean by "whatever comes"? Joe asked.

"You never know. I might be replaced" Don said.

I could tell he was a bit worried even though he did not show it. I went back to my desk.

That evening after having dinner I went for a walk on the beach. I took my shoes and socks off and rolled my pants up and started to walk on soft gritty white sand until the waves started massaging my feet. After walking over a mile I sat on a boulder to listen to waves talk to me. Things are different today. They were not violent in 1960. Why so violent fifteen years later? The waves gave me a fierce roar and almost came up to where I was sitting. I got the answer. The demand for the cocaine and heroin had increased and the guys were going back and forth to the mainland with the product from here. The waves kept roaring were giving me message "Stop the shipments, follow the money". I cleaned off my feet put my socks and shoes on and went back to my apartment

CHAPTER 71

The general elections had passed and the Progressive Party was in power. There were lots of changes in the top personnel in government offices. It has been a while and I have not heard from David. I was wondering if he had been swept out. I did know that Superintendent Calera had retired and the new incumbent was a man named Torrens. It seemed that he had shaken up some of the ranks and transferred some of the brass around.

I went to the office and asked Marta if Don was back from Washington.

"He is in his office", she said.

"Is he in a good mood?" I asked.

"He's alright. He is recovering from the stress of the trip", She said.

"Why are you packing? Are you are you leaving us? I asked.

"We are leaving. Go talk to Don, will you", She said

I went over to Don's office and knocked on the door.

"Come in Robin. Have a seat", Don said.

"How was your meeting in Washington?" I asked.

"We discussed the cases and at the end they seemed pleased we had broken the ring that was exporting hundreds of kilos to the mainland. I also told them the 250 kilos missing were in the Dominican Republic. They said better there than here. They would like us to try to track down the two million that went missing".

"Well I guess congratulations are in order", I said.

"I need you to pack everything. We are moving out of San Juan to the Pan Am building in Hato Rey", Don said.

"When will this take place?" I asked.

"As soon as the movers come and start taking the furniture. Probably by the end of the week", Don said.

"OK. By the way, the interrogations of Santin and Rivera gathered us some good intell. They are trying to get a plea bargain", I said.

"Yes I understand they identified a man working with Revilla. His name is Severiano Hernandez also known as Chumita. He was the contact here in Puerto Rico for the Colombian group from Cali. His contact in Colombia was Rodolfo Madariga. Rodolfo works for the Rodriguez group. The embassy has requested that both, Severiano and Rodolfo, be arrested and extradited", Don said.

"Well, at least it's a step in the right direction. I doubt the Colombian government will comply. The money for the people in Colombia is deposited in Banco Real. The bank manager, Mr. Chelles, did not know that the money was the proceeds of drug transactions. He was told it was from real estate investments", I said.

"Are they charging him with conspiracy to launder money?" Don asked.

"Not yet, they can't prove he was doing anything but depositing the money. We are trying to get Rivera to testify implicating him which he has not done. I am sure it's because he has a bundle of money tied up in that bank. I do have other sources I am exploring", I said

"I am sure he's trying to get a better plea bargain and that might be the reason while he is holding back", Don said.

"We searched his pent house and you should see the luxuries. We also found about a kilo of cocaine in powder puffs in the bathrooms', I said.

"I understand he had parties where friends in high places indulged in it", Don said.

"That is correct. We'll let me go and start packing", I said.

Chapter 72

News of the arrest travels fast in circles of the dealers and users. Some of the dealers stayed off their point of distribution for awhile. Chumita packed it up and went to Colombia and called Calixto.

"So what is going on in Puerto Rico?" Calixto asked.

"The Americans have arrested more than a dozen people and the local Policia is imitating them trying to arrest more" Chumita answered.

"Are you safe? Where are you?" Calixto asked.

"I just arrived here in Bogota I am at the apartment" Chumita responded.

"Well, stay there. I will let Rodolfo know. He might need your services soon", Calixto said.

"OK whatever you say boss. I will talk to you soon then", Chumita hung up.

Jose Antonio came over to talk to Calixto and said, "I got a call from the Commander of the Police in Bogota. The American Embassy has arrest warrants for Rodolfo and Chumita. We have only a couple of hours to get them out of here".

"I have an airplane going out to Guinea Bissau. I'll have them leave at once", Calixto said.

Calixto called Chumita and Rodolfo and told them where to go to get the airplane that was waiting for them.

"They arrested some big shots in Puerto Rico", Jose Antonio said.

"What do you mean by big shots?" Calixto asked.

"You know, some high ranking government officials and some police officers", Jose said.

"I guess we will be losing a little bit of revenue from that area", Calixto said.

"Maybe we can remedy that by air shipping our Tia Nora(cocaine) directly to Miami, using the Medellin connection" Jose said.

"I don't think our father will approve and also it is going to cut into our profits", Calixto said.

"We are selling them over five tons of refined products. It's 97% pure at a very good price which enables us to cut a good deal with them", Jose said.

"Who are you dealing with over there?" Calixto asked.

"Well, Carlos is working the air transport and Fabio and Gonzalo are doing some additional marketing", Jose said

"What is Pablo doing?" Calixto asked

"He is keeping the government officials happy", Jose said.

"So it seems they have it all figured out. How long will it be for them to run us out of business?" Calixto asked.

"I don't think that will happen. You see, the market is growing. The demand for Tia Nora has tripled in the United States and Europe", Jose said.

"Well let's not forget our friends in Mexico. I have also been working with Brazil and Argentina. They have increased their orders also", Calixto said.

"So you see there is enough for all of us to work", Jose said.

"So you say you talked to our father and he says all this is fine", Calixto said.

"Yes I talked to him again after we came back from our fishing trip with these guys and he said it was a good idea to do business with them", Jose said.

"Where is the old man now?" Calixto asked.

"He was in Madrid but he is back in Morocco now", Jose said.

"OK let me get to work. I have to go to the plant and see Jairo", Calixto said.

Chapter 73

We finally got settled to the Pan Am building. Don's office was at the entrance secluded behind the reception counter and secretary area. I was at the end of a long hall in a quad with several desks around me. We were getting ready to receive reinforcements. Joe was supervising the quad with me and Arnaldo the first two on his team. McIntire, Andrew and Jose were in the next quad.

I had managed to get Santin to cooperate. From his information we were able to prosecute the District Court Judge from Humacao, Judge Cardona for conspiracy to sell heroin. He was working with some felons who he had dismissed their cases on grounds of lack of evidence. He was to be disbarred lost his license to practice law. My telephone rang.

"Yes Lidia who is it?"

"It's someone called history something. I could not get the rest. He says he wants to say hello".

"Holy cow, he's alive. OK put him thru".

"Hello Robin. Where have you been hiding all these months", David said.

"We have been awfully busy, David"

"So I read in the San Juan Star. You guys arrested a prosecutor from Ponce and an Assistant Secretary of the Treasure including a bunch of cops also", David said.

"Yes, it has been a lot of work but your tip on this case paid off. What have you been up to?" I asked.

"With the Progressive Party in power now, the focus has changed. We are now chasing subversive radicals. Have you heard what happened at Cerro Maravilla?" David asked.

"Not very much so what's the latest?" I asked.

"Cerro Maravilla you know is the tallest mountain on the Island and that is where most of your agencies and ours have relay communication towers", David said.

"Yes, I know that. Spare me the geography lesson and tell me what happened", I said.

"One of the Macheteros reported to the police that some members were going to go up and blow up the towers. When the two Macheteros arrived at the towers, members of the death squad were waiting. The two Macheteros were executed on site", David said.

"Wow buddy. I had heard a little but I thought it was an exaggeration. So I guess they shot first and ask questions later. One hell of a way to run a country", I said.

"I have to agree. After all it is an imposition to assimilate and have us lose some of our cultural heritage", David said.

"I think you will never lose the cultural heritage. The will of the people is so strong, plus you have over 500 years of heritage. So do you still have your team?" I asked.

"Yes for the moment I have been untouched but you never know what tomorrow will bring", David said.

"Well David I am glad you called, I was going to call you to say good bye. I am leaving tomorrow because my father is ill and I want to spend some time with him and my mother", I said.

"So you are going to New Mexico? I hope everything works out for you. It was a pleasure working with you", David said.

"Thank you it was good working you also. Is Maranda there?" I asked.

"No, she left a while ago. Any messages for her? He asked.

"Nah, I just wanted to say goodbye", I said.

"Not a problem. I will tell her", David said.

"Our mission here has just started and I am sure I will eventually be back here David", I said and hung up.

David went over to Maranda and said, "Randy he's leaving tomorrow morning. I know you are all bent out of shape. Go to the airport and send him off with a hope".

Her eyes were watery and she just shuck her head.

The next morning I caught a taxi to the airport. The radio was on and "Band on the Run" was playing. I noticed the police presence at the Lloren Torres public housing as we passed by. I thought our effort has only taken a small bite out of the big pie. At that rate it is going to take a long time and even then will we achieve victory on this war against drugs. Mi taxi arrived and dropped me off. I noticed a red mustang parked in front of the main terminal. I went in, looked around, and checked in. I walked over to the gate. All of a sudden I heard a voice behind me.

"Were you planning on leaving without saying goodbye", Maranda said.

I turned around and could not take my eyes off of her.

"Are you going to say something? She asked.

"Yes, I am so happy to see you. I am extremely happy to see you. Damn, my heart is beating so quick my words get twisted. I just can't take my eyes off of you", I said.

She came over and held my hand and said "I am happy to see you and sad at the same time"

I held both of her hands and said "I wish I did not have to go but my father . . .", I was interrupted.

"I know, I know. David told me. I just want you to know that . . ."

I interrupted her pulling her close to me and giving her a long kiss. She reciprocated with another.

"I feel for you something that I have not felt for someone in long time. I love you and I want to come back and stay with you", I said.

"From the moment I saw I felt something and I was fighting it because I knew you would be leaving. I do love you and if you don't write or call I will go to New Mexico and bring you back.

They started last call for boarding and we had to kiss again and I finally made it in the airplane.